The Young Mary
Queen of Scots

D0514404

Also available by the same author in Piccolo

THE YOUNG ELIZABETH

The Young Mary
Queen of Scots

Jean Plaidy

Illustrations by William Randell

A Piccolo Book

PAN BOOKS LTD
LONDON

First published in Great Britain 1962
by Macdonald and Co. Ltd.
This edition published 1972 by Pan Books Ltd,
33 Tothill Street, London, S.W.1.

ISBN 0 330 02986 X

Made and printed in Great Britain by
Cox & Wyman Ltd., London, Reading and Fakenham

Contents

1

Danger in Stirling Castle

Five little girls knelt on the window seat and looked out from the schoolroom of Stirling Castle. They were all five years old and all named Mary.

It had been the sort of day when everyone seemed to be expecting something exciting to happen.

'They ought to tell us,' said one of the girls in a rather resentful voice. This was Mary Beaton.

'As Mary is the Queen,' added the girl who was kneeling next to Mary Beaton, and whose name was Mary Fleming, 'she should know everything that happens in the Castle.'

'Not only in the Castle,' added Mary Livingstone, the third girl, 'but everywhere in Scotland.'

The tallest of the children suddenly leaped from the window seat and, putting her head on one side, regarded her four companions with amusement.

'And as I am your Queen, Livy,' she said with a hint of imperiousness which they knew was not to be taken seriously, '*you* should not tell *me* what I ought to do. Nor should you, Flem. All the same,' she added, 'it's true that as I am the Queen I ought to know.'

This was Mary Stuart who a few weeks after her birth had become Queen of Scotland and the Isles, when her father, James V of Scotland, had been killed at the battle of Solway Moss.

Mary's mother had often told her how she had been crowned when she was only nine months and one day old, and how the great noblemen of Scotland had bowed before the baby and sworn allegiance to Mary, Queen of Scotland and the Isles.

Some girls might have felt over-awed by the responsibility of such royal rank, but Mary was not serious by nature; she loved to laugh and make everyone about her happy even though, because of her friendly, affectionate and generous nature, they sometimes forgot to pay her the homage due to someone in such an important position.

Now she threw back her long reddish brown curls and flashed on all of them her most fascinating smile because she was afraid she might have spoken a little too sharply to Flem and Livy. She saw that Mary Seton was watching her silently. Mary Seton was the quiet one, but nevertheless – and perhaps because of this – the one who saw most. She might very well know the cause of the tension which for some weeks had existed in the Castle.

'I think I shall ask my mother,' said the little Queen.

'If she had wished you to know she would have told you already,' Mary Beaton reminded her.

'Perhaps,' went on the Queen, 'it is something which

is not very pleasant, and in that case it is better not to know.'

A clatter of horses' hoofs below sent the five girls back to the window again, where they watched a small party of horsemen, riding into the Castle courtyard, and the grooms who came to take their horses.

'They are English,' said Mary Beaton. 'You can see from their livery, and depend upon it, they come with messages from the King of England.'

'Then,' said Mary Stuart, 'perhaps we are friends again with the English. But I shall never like them because they killed my father.'

Livy, who hated serious conversation, picked up her shuttlecock which was lying on the floor and began batting it into the air. Flem watched her and then ran for her battledore and shuttlecock. The three others looked on with interest at the match which was taking place, waiting for the first of the feathery shuttlecocks to fall to the floor.

'Flem will win,' said Mary Beaton. 'Livy gets too excited.' And sure enough at that moment Livy failed to catch the shuttlecock on her battledore.

The Queen took up her own battledore. 'Come,' she cried. 'We will all play and I shall beat every one of you.'

In a few seconds the room was full of the plop-plop of shuttlecocks hitting battledores – a pleasant peaceful sound which the little Queen was to remember for a long time because, looking back later it seemed like the end of one phase of her life.

The door opened suddenly and the Queen's governess came into the room. This was Lady Fleming, mother of Flem and a distant relation of the royal House of Scotland. She was a beautiful woman with masses of reddish gold hair, and remarkably like her little daughter. The children went on playing after they had seen who it was, for none of them was the least bit in awe of her; she was the least strict of governesses, rarely scolded them and was always ready to make excuses for any misdemeanours; indeed it

was very easy for someone with Mary's charm to wheedle
what she wanted from Lady Fleming.

Now the governess clapped her hands.

'Come now, children,' she said, 'I have something to say to
you.'

The shuttlecocks fluttered to the floor and the five Marys
made a little circle about Lady Fleming, whose eyes went
from her own daughter to the Queen.

'How hot you look!' she cried, clicking her tongue. 'Your
hair is so untidy. And the Queen Mother is asking that you
be sent to her without delay!'

Mary smoothed down her hair and tried to look demure;
she always felt that she was the one who must take care of
Lady Fleming – which was a strange way to feel about one's
governess. If her mother was inclined to criticize the manner
in which Lady Fleming managed the nursery, Mary would
always have an excuse ready.

She knew that her governess was like her daughter – Flem,
somewhat feckless, liking to laugh, turning away from anything which might be unpleasant – in fact just a little frivolous.

Perhaps, thought Mary, I am rather like that myself.

'Why does she want to see me?' asked Mary.

'Now that is something she will wish to tell you herself.'

'I suppose you do not know,' Mary added; 'but I wonder if
it has anything to do with the messengers who have been
coming to the Castle all day.'

Lady Fleming pursed her lips and tried to look wise. If she
really knew, it would not be difficult to prise the secret from
her; but Mary was sure that her governess knew very little
more than she and her Marys had been able to find out.

'They are English,' said Flem, 'and Mary hates the English.'

'It is wrong to hate anyone,' Lady Fleming retorted. 'And
Her Majesty said that you were to present yourself to her
without delay. But come here. How crumpled your gown is!
What will she say!'

Mary smiled, and her smile always made people pause to look at her, because it was dazzling.

'Never mind, dear Lady Fleming,' she said, 'I shall tell her how shocked you were because I looked so untidy, and how you wanted me to change my gown and I refused.'

'She will tell me that I have no control over you,' Lady Fleming wailed.

'I'll tell her that you are a very stern governess.'

'Alas, she would not believe you,' Lady Fleming answered with a grimace. 'Now, you must go to your mother at once. You have already delayed too long.'

Mary saw that her four friends were watching her with a new respect. It was at times like this that they remembered that she was their Queen; at others she was just a playmate – a little more self-assertive than the rest of them, one who was the leader in all their games, more because of her nature, than the fact that she was their Queen.

Soberly she shut the door and hurried to her mother's private apartments.

What was it going to be this time? A lecture on the importance of her position? Or perhaps stories of her grand relations in France? This was what she preferred, and she secretly believed that there was nothing her mother liked discussing more than those long ago days of *her* childhood which had been spent in France with that noble family which, according to her, was the most important not only in France but in the whole world – the Guises.

Mary knew that across the sea, in the land of France, she had a very important grandfather who was the Duke of Guise, and her French grandmother was Antoinette de Bourbon; and through them she was closely related to the French royal family. She had six uncles of whom her mother spoke as though they were gods. They were all tall and handsome as, it seemed, only the Guises could be. The two most important of these uncles were Uncle Francis and Uncle Charles – one a soldier, the other a man of the Church.

'Men such as your uncles,' her mother had said, 'are the true rulers.'

Everything that was most beautiful in this Palace of Stirling – or in Linlithgow where Mary had been born – had come from France. The silken hangings, the delicately embroidered upholstery, the pictures, the beautiful dresses and jewels which her mother wore – they all came from France.

One day, thought Mary, I shall go to France. I shall see my wonderful uncles, and I shall be as happy as my mother was there.

In her apartments the Queen Mother was impatiently awaiting the arrival of her daughter and, as the little girl entered and she watched her intently, there was a faint frown on her face, but she could not maintain this for long.

Mary had been slow in coming; she had not combed her hair; her dress was crumpled; but none of this could detract from her beauty. Mary was the loveliest child her mother – or anyone else at the Scottish Court – had ever seen. Her eyes were deeply set and slightly darker than her hair; her face, plump and round, still showed signs of babyhood; when she had lost her baby-fat it would be a perfect oval; but it was not her features which were so enchanting; nor was it the delicately tinted skin; it was the latent gaiety always ready to bubble over; the mobile expression which could change in a second from joy to sorrow; and the sorrow would be as deep for someone else as it would be for herself. Mary had so much affection that she longed to shower it upon everyone around her.

'May the saints preserve my lovely daughter,' prayed the Queen Mother, and taking Mary in her arms held her tightly against her for a few seconds. When she released her, her face had grown stern again.

'You were long in coming. Did not your governess tell you I was waiting?'

'Oh yes, Mother, she told me I must hurry. It was my fault that I was so long. And Lady Fleming told me to make myself clean and tidy.'

The Queen Mother suppressed her smile. 'You are very fond of your governess,' she said.

'She is so kind to us all; and then of course she is Flem's mother.'

'Flem!' murmured the Queen Mother reprovingly.

'Mary Fleming. If I call her Mary, and Livy Mary, and Seton and Beaton all Mary, how can we know which is which? So I have to give them other names.'

'How inconsiderate of your friends' parents to give them all the same name as yours!' said the Queen Mother with a smile. 'It would have been so much easier if there had been a Janet or Jean among them.'

'Oh no, Mother,' replied Mary earnestly, 'I am glad they are all Marys. It makes them seem so very much my own friends. I have promised them that they shall always be with me wherever I go.'

A shadow passed over the Queen Mother's face. 'You should not make promises, my dear, when you cannot be sure that you can honour them.'

'But I *will* honour them,' replied Mary warmly. 'I have promised that where I go they shall go, and so they shall. I am the Queen.'

Her mother was momentarily startled. She could see her brother Francis in the child at that moment. So might he have spoken. Yet in spite of Mary's occasional arrogance there was much softness in her nature, and it was this side of her character which would make her vulnerable.

'That is for the future,' said the Queen Mother.

'But is not everything for the future, Mother?'

'Yes, my child; but some events are far away and others press close.'

Now it was coming: the reason for the summons to her mother's apartment, the reason for the tension in the Castle.

Mary waited attentively.

'You have seen messengers arriving at the Castle. They come from the King of England.'

Mary caught her breath and a solemn expression came into her face.

'I know what you are thinking,' said her mother. 'Should we receive the English here, when it was English soldiers who killed your father? Mary, there is much you will have to learn, and learn quickly. Quarrels are mended and the quickest way in which quarrels between countries can be mended is by uniting families in marriage – so that enemies become friends. Do you understand?'

'Yes, Mother,' said Mary.

'You have been learning your lessons, I hope, and in particular what is happening in the countries near your own. Tell me, who is the King of England?'

'It is King Henry VIII, and it was his army which—' began Mary impetuously, but the Queen Mother held up a hand to silence her.

'I have not summoned you here to mourn for the past but to plan for the future. The King of England has a son, a boy not much older than you.'

'Prince Edward,' Mary put in.

'That is so. And the King of England believes that there could be peace between his country and ours if his son, who will one day be King of England, married you who are already the Queen of Scotland.'

'So I am to be married!'

'Hush, hush! You go too fast. You will not be married until you are of an age to be so. That will be in some ten years' time.'

'But I am to be married to Prince Edward?' persisted Mary.

Her mother did not speak for a few seconds and Mary realized, from her expression, that she was wondering how much she dared to tell her daughter.

The Queen Mother laid her hand on Mary's head. 'You will hear talk in the Castle,' she said, 'and there may be some who will try to persuade you that it would be an excellent thing for you to go to England, to become Queen of England as well as Scotland.'

'And you do not think so, Mother?'

'When I think of your marriage, my daughter,' said the Queen Mother slowly, as though she were speaking to herself, 'I do not think of England.'

Mary had a flash of understanding. 'You think of France!' she said.

Her mother looked over her shoulder as though she feared someone might be hiding in the arras. She said in a whisper: 'You are right. I think of France. The King of France has a son even as the King of England has and they are both heirs to their fathers' crowns.'

Mary was aware of her mother's unhappiness and immediately sought to soothe it. 'But it is all so far away,' she said. 'It will not be for years and years—'

'Mary, I do not wish you to speak to anyone of what I am about to say to you – not even your Marys. I would not speak of it to you even, if I did not feel that it is necessary to do so. Will you give me your word that you will say nothing to anyone?'

'I promise, Mother,' answered Mary solemnly.

'Then listen to me. Many of the people in this country of ours are not of our religion. They are Protestants and it is the desire of many of the nobles of this Court to make a Protestant of you, their Queen. That must never be. It is for this reason that they would prefer to see you married to the Protestant Prince of England rather than the Catholic Dauphin of France. They would do a great deal to bring this about. In fact they would—'

Her mother did not finish her sentence but Mary understood. She knew that sometimes people suffered death for their religious opinions. She was vaguely aware of a new danger surrounding her. Her mother would never have spoken to her in this way if it had not been close.

'Mary, I want you to listen to what is said to you. If Lords Arran or Douglas should speak to you of the English marriage, I want you to listen to what they have to say and come straight to me and tell me about it. Will you do this?'

'Yes, Mother.'

'And offer no opinion. If they should praise Prince Edward to you, tell them that you are too young to think of marriage. You see, I am eager to keep you with me. It is the wish of the King of England that you should leave Scotland and go to England, there to be brought up as his own daughter.'

'Go to England!'

'Do not be alarmed. You are not to go. I will never allow it.'

'But why should I go to England when it will be years before I could marry?'

'Because, my child, the King of England wishes you to be brought up as his daughter; he wants you to have the manners of an English girl, not a Scottish one. There are men at this Court who are more the friends of the English than of us.'

Mary could not understand. She had thought the English were their most bitter enemies. Constantly she had heard of how the English raided the towns and villages on the Border and carried off the sheep and cattle. How strange that her country's enemy should wish to take Scotland's Queen and make an English girl of her. But the world of adults at times seemed topsy-turvy and she could not understand it at all. At the same time she was wise enough to know that her mother was warning her, that she was frightened that some of the powerful men, who on state occasions kissed her hand and swore allegiance to her, might betray her to the English.

The Queen Mother was frowning. How can one explain to such a child, she asked herself. I ask too much of my daughter. I am forcing her to grow up before she is ready.

But what else could she do? There was peril in Stirling Castle; it threatened the Queen; she must be put on her guard.

She thought of the King of England who was no longer young. He was eager for a marriage between his son and Mary, Queen of Scots. And what he most desired was that Mary should go to England and be brought up in his Court.

On the surface it seemed a reasonable enough request. The King of France, had he decided on a match between Mary and the Dauphin, might have made the same request. But there was a difference. If Mary went to France she would have her powerful relations, the Guises, to watch over her. In England she would be surrounded by enemies and there would be none to protect her.

Moreover there was a clause in the agreement which would have to be signed if Mary were betrothed to Prince Edward. It was that if Mary should die even before the wedding took place, the crown of Scotland should pass to England.

The Queen Mother had shuddered when she read that clause. The King of England had killed many who stood in his way, including two of his wives. So why should he hesitate to remove a girl who would be completely friendless and in his power?

Never, never must Mary be allowed to go to England.

Nor should she, if it depended on her mother. But did it depend on her? These Scottish nobles had never taken kindly to Mary of Guise; they resented what they called her Frenchified ways, and was she not trying to bring up her daughter to be exactly like herself? That was what they said; and she knew that many of them were secretly in league with the English.

It might be that one day they would seek to kidnap the Queen, to carry her off across the Border, to the Court of the English King who did not hesitate to murder those who stood in his way.

But how explain all this to a girl of five?

So the Queen Mother warned her daughter as best she could. She would redouble her vigil. Alas, how could she know who were to be trusted?

'So,' she went on, 'it is my wish that you should stay in Scotland. You must be more discreet, my daughter. You must learn to listen when others speak and to guard your tongue.'

Mary threw herself into her mother's arms – not because she was afraid for herself, but because she sensed her mother's fear and longed to comfort her.

'Do not worry, Mother,' she said. 'No one shall take me away from you.'

The Queen Mother stooped and kissed the soft cheek.

'Please tell me about my Grandmamma de Bourbon and Grandpapa who is the great Duke of Guise.'

The Queen Mother held the child against her and was soon telling of her childhood and the magnificence of the Duke, her father, and the honour of belonging to the family of Guise and Lorraine.

Mary soon forgot the strange conversation which had just taken place, and in her imagination was in the great château which was her grandparents' home; but the Queen Mother was not thinking of the past as she talked with her daughter; she could not throw off her fear.

She could sense peril all about her – menacing the peace of Stirling Castle and perhaps the life of the Queen of Scots.

2

Flight from Stirling

The five Marys sat at lessons but none of them was paying much attention. Lady Fleming, who should have been with them, had not appeared that day and even Flem did not know where she was. It was not easy to concentrate on lessons when there was no one to watch over them and answer any questions.

They were talking about the English. It seemed to Mary that in Stirling Castle people talked more about the English than anything else.

Mary spoke her thoughts aloud: 'Since his old father died, Edward is King of England.'

Beaton who prided herself on knowing the latest news said: 'I hear he is very delicate and will not live long. Who will be King of England if Edward dies?'

'He is too young to die,' said Mary. 'He is only a boy really.'

'And that is why there is a Lord Protector of England to rule until Edward is old enough to do so himself,' added the knowledgeable Beaton. 'And if he *should* die, he has a sister who would be Queen.'

'He has two sisters,' said Mary, 'one with our name and another called Elizabeth.'

'They are only half-sisters,' Beaton explained. 'But we shall never be friends with the English. They are fighting again.'

'Have you noticed,' asked the Queen, looking round her as though she expected to see something that was not there, 'that it is very quiet in the Castle today?'

'It is often quiet,' said Beaton.

'No, it is different today. I have not seen my mother. But I believe she called a meeting in her audience chamber and that all those who went are still with her.'

'It has something to do with the war,' said Beaton. 'Depend upon it.'

'Perhaps there is to be peace,' suggested Mary. 'Oh, I do hope so. Wars make everyone so unhappy. It is certainly strange that Lady Fleming has not come to see how we are getting on with our lessons.'

Flem rose from her seat and said: 'I could go and ask my mother.'

'Yes,' said Mary, smiling mischievously because she was aware that if something secret was going on, and Lady Fleming knew of it, it would not be difficult to wheedle the knowledge from her. 'Let us all go to Lady Fleming's apartment.'

With Mary leading the way, they went quietly from the

schoolroom and through corridors and up spiral staircases until they came to Lady Fleming's apartment.

Mary tapped lightly on the door, and as there was no answer opened it very cautiously, and tiptoed into the room followed by her four companions.

As she did so a figure rose from a stool, and it was difficult in those first seconds to recognize in that sad, dejected person the usually gay and lighthearted Lady Fleming.

'Mother!' cried Flem. Lady Fleming turned slowly and seeing her daughter held out her arms and Flem ran to her; clung together, and the four Marys looked on aghast as they heard the sound of sobbing.

Mary knew then that something dreadful had happened; and could no longer restrain her feelings; she ran to Lady Fleming and tried to put her arms about her. 'Dear Lady Fleming,' she said, 'is there anything I can do to help you?'

Lady Fleming shook her head. 'You are too young to understand. But you will soon hear. We have been routed at the battle of Pinkie Cleugh. Fourteen thousand of our men have fallen there, among them – my husband. I am a widow now, Your Majesty, and my daughter is fatherless. I am no fit companion for you, so take your three Marys away and leave my daughter here with me.'

Mary nodded gravely and, with Beaton, Seton and Livy, went away leaving Flem to comfort her mother.

Back in the schoolroom Mary sat silently smoothing the folds of her wine-coloured velvet gown.

They did not speak because they could think of nothing but poor little Flem who had no father now. Suddenly Beaton, who was kneeling on the window seat, cried: 'Look!' In a second the little girls were kneeling beside her. They saw the messenger riding into the Castle courtyard; it was clear that he had ridden far for both he and his horse looked exhausted; his clothes were torn and stained with mud, and the horse was flecked with foam.

'He brings bad news,' cried Seton.

'I am going to find out what it is,' said Mary, running to the door of the schoolroom. The three Marys followed her; but she turned to them and explained: 'So many of us would be seen. Leave this to me.'

She left them and ran to the great staircase. Looking between the pillars of the balustrade she saw the messenger in the hall. The sound of excited voices was carried up to her; she recognized those of the Earl of Arran and Lord Erskine with that of Livy's father, Lord Livingstone.

The messenger was saying: 'My lords, I came with all speed. Hertford's men cannot be more than six miles from the Castle.'

Lord Livingstone said: 'The Queen Mother must be told without delay.'

They were coming up the stairs with the messenger; Mary turned and fled, and did not stop running until she was back in the schoolroom.

That night Mary was awakened by the sound of voices and a flickering light in her room, and for a few seconds she lay wondering whether she was dreaming.

'Is the child still asleep?' That was her mother's voice.

'Yes, Your Majesty.' That was Lord Livingstone.

'We must awaken her. There is no time to lose.'

'The horses will be ready in less than five minutes.'

'And so shall she.'

Mary started up and saw her mother's face in the light of the candles.

'Mother!' she cried.

'There is nothing to fear, my child. You are going to leave your bed and dress as quickly as possible.'

'It is night time!'

'That is so. But you are leaving Stirling.'

'But why?'

'This is no time for questions. Janet, where are you? Help the Queen to dress. Quickly. We must be leaving in a few minutes.'

Mary then saw Lady Fleming at the bedside.

'Aunt Janet—'

'Hush, my dear. There is little time left to us.'

Mary felt bewildered while her clothes were hastily put on; she could see that the Earl of Arran and Lord Erskine were with Livy's father; they were standing together in a corner of the room, speaking in whispers and looking agitated.

'Are we running away?'

Lady Fleming nodded.

'From the English,' whispered Mary; and then she remembered the words of the messenger: 'Hertford's men are six miles from the Castle.' Lord Hertford was Lord Protector of England, who ruled because King Edward was not old enough to do so; and Hertford's men had defeated the Scots at the battle of Pinkie Cleugh, at which poor Flem had lost her father.

It was becoming clear. If Mary did not run away they would make *her* their prisoner; perhaps they would kill her as they had poor Flem's father.

'Is the child ready?'

Lady Fleming was wrapping Mary's fur-trimmed cape about her and drawing the hood over her head. 'All ready now, Your Majesty.'

Mary's hand was in that of her mother as she was hustled down the great staircase, through the hall and out into the courtyard where the horses were stamping.

Her mother lifted her in her arms, and for a moment Mary thought she would never let her go; she felt a swift kiss on her forehead.

'Mother,' she cried, 'you are coming with me?'

Her mother did not answer and at that moment she was lifted in a pair of strong arms which she believed belonged to Livy's father; she could not clearly see because it was dark, and light from the torch was not shining her way.

She was seated on a horse and someone in the saddle was holding her firmly in her place.

She heard her mother's voice. 'Remember – you carry the Queen.'

That was all. She was being borne away from Stirling Castle and she did not know whither.

She wanted to ask questions, but this was not possible as she was carried along on the galloping horse. It was very dark, and she was worn out by all the excitement of this strange day. She could smell the mist and feel her own heart beating as she wondered who was riding with them.

Hertford is after us, she thought. He wants to make me his prisoner. That is why we are running away.

She thought of her four little friends and cried out: 'Are my Marys with me? I must have my Marys with me.'

But nobody answered her, so perhaps no one heard.

She listened to the thudding of hoofs and as she swayed with the horse the events of that strange day became jumbled in her mind; her thoughts became confused; she was not sure whether she was really riding away from the Caste or whether she was dreaming it.

And thus she slept.

When she awoke she was lying on what seemed like a hard bed; she could hear whispering voices and a sound which she did not recognize for a few moments.

Then she knew. It was that of oars dipping into water.

'Where am I?' she cried.

And immediately a cool hand was laid on her forehead.

'All is well,' said a voice. 'I am with you.'

'Aunt Janet!' she whispered.

Lady Fleming bent over her and kissed her.

'It is so dark,' said Mary.

'Sometimes,' answered Lady Fleming, 'we must thank the saints for the darkness.'

There were so many questions which Mary wanted to ask, but she was so tired that she could not keep her eyes open; however, the fact that her governess was beside her made her feel safe.

She woke again when she was lifted from the boat. She was

fleetingly aware of a figure in a monk's robe who lifted her in his arms.

'Who are you?' she asked sleepily.

'I am the Abbot, my child. You should return to your sleep. You are safe now – safe on the island of Inchmahome.'

3

On the Isle of Inchmahome

Mary awoke next morning to the sound of a bell's ringing. She was lying on a narrow pallet which could scarcely be called a bed, and she was alone in a narrow room with cold-looking walls bare of everything but a crucifix.

She started up wondering where she was and then immediately she remembered her ride through the night. Leaping out of bed, she looked about her and noticed at once that there were no rugs or even rushes on the cold stone floor. Nothing could be in greater contrast to her apartments at Stirling Castle, and for a few moments she felt such a wave of nostalgia that she was ready to burst into tears.

Very soon, however, natural curiosity overcame that emotion and she ran to the window which was merely a narrow slit in the wall. She stood on a stool to climb up to this, and through it she could see part of the grey building in which she was now housed, and grassy land which ran down to the water. Her eyes went to the tranquil blue of the lake. Of one thing she was certain – she was a long way from home.

As she was clambering down from her stool the door opened and Lady Fleming came into the cell.

'So you are awake already,' she said.

'The bell awakened me.'

'As it did me. Oh dear, I wonder how we are going to like living in this place! I feel as though every bone in my body is broken, after that dreadful ride last night – or I should say this morning.'

'Where are the Marys sleeping?' asked Mary.

Her governess looked at her sadly. 'In Stirling Castle, safely and peacefully, I hope.'

Mary cried in alarm: 'They did not come with us?'

'My dear, we left hurriedly. There was one thought only in our minds: to bring you to safety.'

'I know the English were not far off and they wanted to make me their prisoner, but I cannot stay here without my Marys.'

Lady Fleming did not answer, and Mary immediately understood that although she was the Queen she would have to obey the orders of her mother and her guardians; and this might well mean that, even though she commanded that her Marys be brought to her, she could command in vain.

She was angry because she could not imagine how she could bear to be cut off from them for a very long time. 'They *shall* come,' she said. 'I am the Queen, and I shall *demand* that they do. Where are we now?'

'At Inchmahome – an island in the Lake of Menteith. We are to stay here in the monastery, where the monks will look after us until the danger is past. You should be thankful that we reached here in safety.'

'I want my friends with me,' Mary explained. 'How can I be thankful when I must wonder all day what is happening to them?'

Lady Fleming shook her head sadly; and then Mary remembered her governess's recent grief, and reproached herself for thinking of her own sorrows when those of her governess were so much greater.

How long the days seemed! Life was punctuated by the bell. Regularly throughout the day it rang out. Mary soon knew when to expect it and she was always glad to hear it rung for Compline which meant that that was the end of another day.

She was now accustomed to seeing the black-clad figures of the monks gliding through those silent corridors; they gave her gentle smiles but they did not speak to her until she spoke to them; they all seemed so busy, for each had his task, and gradually she grew to know them by their names and the work they did. She would go into the bakeries and watch the making of bread; she would sit in the gardens and watch the bent figures as they hoed and weeded.

One day as she came back from a walk and entered the monastery precincts she met the Abbot; he was coming from the chapel on his way to the monks' dorter when he saw her sadly strolling across the grassy courtyard.

He gave her his gentle smile and said: 'You are lonely, are you not? You do not like to be a prisoner on our island?'

Mary politely tried to think of what she did like about the monastery and said: 'There is greater peace here than there was in Stirling Castle; and because we are surrounded by water we feel safe.'

'Yet the days seem twice as long in Inchmahome?' he asked. 'And there is nothing that happens except the ringing of the bell from Matins to Compline. Bells which summon us to prayer. Yet we are happy here, my Queen.'

'You are monks,' she said wisely, 'and you have chosen this life.'

'But do you know why we are happy here? It is because we have so much to do. We work for each other. Each of us has his task and each task is for the good of the community. There are brothers who tend the gardens; others who feed us; some who clean for us; a few are engaged on making illuminated manuscripts which will be a credit to our monastery when we are all no more. That is why we can be happy in Inchmahome. But you find the days long because you have nothing to do. Now suppose I teach you to read and write in Latin, in French and Italian; and you are allowed to go into the kitchens and learn how to bake bread? Suppose you learned what herbs to plant at certain times and what healing qualities these possessed? Would that make you happy?'

May was thoughtful, then she said: 'I should like to learn but I shall never be happy while my four friends are in Stirling and I am in Inchmahome.'

'Tell me of your friends,' said the Abbot.

He listened sympathetically and Mary made up her mind that she would take his advice.

A week later Mary was feeling a little more contented. She was taking lessons in French, Latin, Spanish and Italian; and she learned quickly. On those days when the monastery baking houses were full of the smell of newly-made bread, Mary was there, watching and giving a hand. She was often to be seen gathering herbs, and she delighted in making cures for the ailments of the monks.

But still she fretted. Often she would say: 'I wonder what Flem is doing now. *They* are lucky. They are all together.'

She was allowed to wander where she liked on the island

which was very small: but there were few games one could play alone; and she would often lie in the long grass gazing towards the mainland, thinking of carefree days when she and her Marys had played together, never dreaming of being separated.

Mary sometimes gathered leaves and flowers to take back to the monastery that she might ask Brother Aloysius (who knew more about plants than anyone else at the monastery) what healing properties, if any, they possessed. Mary always hoped to discover something which had never been known before. This desire added zest to her walks – and was a game which could be played by oneself.

One day when Mary was in the herb garden Lady Fleming came to look for her.

'The Abbot wishes to see you without delay,' she said, with a satisfied smile. 'He has a surprise for you.'

Mary leaped up. 'What sort of surprise?'

'You must come and see.'

'Where is he?'

'In the great hall.'

'Goodbye, Brother Aloysius,' said Mary. 'I shall see you later.'

She noticed the same smile of satisfaction on Brother Aloysius's face as she had seen on that of Lady Fleming. So he too was in this secret. Mary felt rather resentful.

'You have some secret which you are trying to keep from me,' she said.

'Well!' murmured Lady Fleming. 'How inquisitive you are growing. Is that becoming in a Queen?'

'I care not,' said Mary hotly. 'I am displeased when everyone knows this secret and keeps me in the dark.'

'The Abbot is waiting for you.'

'Tell me the secret and I will go to him.'

'But the Abbot is waiting, and there is no time for gossiping now.'

Lady Fleming began to walk quickly in the direction of that door which led to the great hall.

As Mary followed, her face was flushed with anger, but when she reached the hall she paused in amazement. For a second or so she thought she was dreaming. Standing with the Abbot were four girls, all wearing travelling cloaks, and because their fur-trimmed hoods had been thrown back Mary saw at once that they were Flem, Livy, Beaton and Seton.

'My Marys!' cried Mary.

There was a spontaneous and simultaneous cry of delight as the four turned and saw their Queen.

How happy she was now on the island of Inchmahome! No longer did she sit alone in the common room doing her lessons. Now the four Marys sat with her; no longer must she roam alone on the island, wondering what was happening to her friends in Stirling Castle. Hide-and-seek was an exciting game when there was an entire island to play it on – not to mention a monastery. No one reproved them when they hid in the monks' dorter or in the bakehouse, the kitchens and cellars. Sometimes it was possible to enlist the help of the monks in these games. Brother James was quite willing to cover his Queen with a heap of hay when it was her turn to hide; Brother Matthew had been known to shut a Mary in one of the great ovens – when it was not in use, of course.

It seemed like an enchanted island now that she had her Marys with her.

Lady Fleming, delighted to have her daughter once more in her care, grew even more easy-going than she had been in Stirling Castle.

Lessons were solemn occasions, but Mary had always enjoyed learning, and the monks were no hard task-masters. They all seemed delighted to have their little Queen on their island.

Those were wonderful days, when the sun seemed to shine all the time, and if the mists rose and the rain came – as they occasionally did – what could be a better playground than a monastery!

Mary began to love the sound of the bell and chanting voices. The four Marys, delighted to be with her, declared that they liked living at Inchmahome better than anywhere else.

They knew of course that Lady Fleming yearned to go back to the mainland. She was becoming reconciled to her widowhood, and Mary believed that she secretly grieved because here on the island there were no balls and banquets and all the gaieties that were a part of Court life.

Mary thought of this when she pinned on her golden agraffe which held her scarf in position. The scarf was brilliant, being of the Stuart tartan; but it was the agraffe which reminded her, every time she pinned it on, of life far away from Inchmahome.

This agraffe came from France and, like so many of Mary's possessions, was a gift from the Guises. On the ornament were the silver eagles of Lorraine, the double cross of Jerusalem and the lilies of Anjou and Sicily. Her mother had said when she had first pinned it on her little daughter's scarf: 'This will always remind you that you belong to the House of Guise and Lorraine.' And Mary always did remember, and even on the island thought of those important uncles of hers who lived far away in France and who, her mother had assured her, would always save her from the wicked English.

When she and her companions were tired they would sit with their backs against the granite walls of the monastery looking out to the lake, and they would talk of what they would do on the next day, and of all the matters of interest which were going on in the monastery. What would the Abbot think of their Latin exercise? Would Brother Aloysius let them taste the brew he was teaching them to make? Would Brother James bake bread on Tuesday instead of Wednesday this week because the ovens had been too hot last Saturday and some of the loaves were baked to a cinder?

Flem suddenly cried out that as Mary had been fingering

her agraffe it was undone and if she did not take care she might lose it.

Mary gravely took off the agraffe and studied the emblem of Guise and Lorraine.

She said sadly: 'I do not think we shall be able to stay here for ever.'

'But why not?' asked Livy, who loved the island dearly because to her it represented a place where trouble could not come.

'Because,' said Mary, 'there are people who will have other plans for me.'

'We shall have to stay here,' put in Beaton, 'until the English have been driven back beyond the Border.'

'They will never let you leave the island while there are Englishmen in Scotland,' added Flem.

Just then they caught sight of Lady Fleming who had come to look for them. When she saw them she waved – not in the least like a lady governess but more as though she were an elder sister. She sat down with them, leaning against the granite wall. 'Do you know when we shall return to the mainland, Aunt Janet?' asked Mary.

'When plans have been completed.'

'Plans! What plans?'

Lady Fleming lifted her shoulders and tried to look innocent. She was about to rise to her feet when the five girls leaped upon her holding her down.

'You must tell – you must tell,' chanted Mary; and the others took up the cry.

'Oh well,' said Lady Fleming. 'You'll have to know one day. Sit down quietly and I'll tell all I can.' When they had obeyed, she went on: 'Now as you know the Lord Protector's men were within a few miles of the Castle, and the English planned to take you to London to be brought up with Prince Edward – so that you could one day marry him. But your mother would not allow that because she has other plans for you. One day, Mary, you will not only be Queen of Scotland but Queen of France.'

'Queen of France!' whispered Mary.

'Oh yes, Queen of France. Secret messages have been going back and forth for a long time. But there are many at the Court who want you for Prince Edward. That shall not be. It is the crown of France for you, my pretty one.'

The four Marys were silent, looking at their Queen who read their thoughts at once.

'You need have no fear,' she said. 'When I go to France you shall come with me. I shall refuse to go anywhere unless I have you all with me.'

The door of Mary's cell was thrown open, and Flem ran in followed by Beaton.

They were white and trembling.

'The English are coming!' cried Flem.

Mary was about to clamber on to her stool to look out of the window, when the Abbot followed by several of the brothers came hurrying into the cell.

'Come along,' said the Abbot, taking Mary's hand. 'There are boats on the lake. At any moment they may be here.'

'The English!' breathed Mary.

Then she saw the agitated face of her governess, and behind her were Seton and Livy. They looked scared.

The Abbot however was calm. 'Now, Lady Fleming,' he said, 'take the Queen and her attendants down to the cellars. Go quickly – and wait there until you hear that you may emerge. Meanwhile I will go out to meet whoever it is who is visiting us. Brother Aloysius will conduct you to the secret tunnels where you should not be discovered. Are they all here? Praise the saints, they are. Go quickly now.'

Grasping Mary with one hand and Flem with the other, Lady Fleming followed Brother Aloysius; the others were close at their heels. Down a long spiral staircase they went, being careful to hold the rope at the side as the stairs were steep and narrow. Round and round they went until they came to the cellars, and then into the dank tunnels which smelt of the lake.

'What if the English take the monastery and stay there for ever!' said Seton.

'We shall live in the tunnels for the rest of our lives,' put in Beaton.

Livy began to cry quietly but Mary said: 'What nonsense! My mother would send for my uncles. They would come across the sea to rescue us.'

'The English are so strong,' sobbed Livy.

'But my uncles are the Guises,' retorted Mary, 'and no one can stand out against them!'

Flustered and excited, Lady Fleming led them into the tunnels; and there Brother Aloysius assured them that if they remained quiet no one would ever find them. He would bring them food as soon as he could.

So he left them, and in the dank cold tunnels Mary began to wonder what would happen next.

She did not have to wait long. Very soon the Abbot himself appeared; he was carrying a lantern which he held high and which showed up the slimy walls of the tunnels.

He was smiling, and yet there was a certain sadness in his smile.

'A false alarm,' he explained. 'They are our friends who have come, not foes.'

Mary was at his side, and he laid a hand on her head as he continued: 'Messengers from your mother.'

'Then that is good, is it not?' asked Mary.

'It is very good, my Queen.'

'But why do you look sad?'

'Do I look sad?' the Abbot asked. 'Perhaps that is because this visit can mean one thing.'

Mary said no more. She understood that it meant: 'Good-bye to Inchmahome.'

4

Across the Sea to France

Mary was in tears as she looked at all those who had come to the shore of the island to say goodbye.

There was the Abbot who, old and wise as he was, could not hide his sorrow while Brother Aloysius unashamedly wiped his eyes.

'One day,' said Mary, 'I shall come back to stay with you.'

'We shall remember you said that,' the Abbot answered; and Mary knew that he did not believe she ever would.

'But I shall,' she insisted.

He knelt so that his face was on a level with hers.

'Dear little Queen,' he said, 'there was a time when we gave you shelter. If you should need a refuge again, always remember Inchmahome is your home. But let us pray that that will not be. For you are a Queen and we are monks, and our paths lie in different directions.'

Lady Fleming was at her side, impatient to be gone.

'They are waiting for Your Majesty to board the boat.'

'Farewell, dear Abbot,' whispered Mary and, to the astonishment of all, she made a most unqueenly gesture by flinging her arms about his neck.

Then it was the turn of dear Brother Aloysius, and Mary was now sobbing piteously.

But Lady Fleming drew her away, whispering that the four Marys were already aboard; and there was nothing the Queen could do but join them.

So Mary obeyed her governess and stood in the rocking boat, waving to the Abbot and the monks, watching them grow smaller and smaller in the distance.

'Farewell, dear Abbot,' she murmured. 'Farewell, dear Inchmahome.'

Stirling Castle seemed bigger and more formidable than Mary remembered it. Her mother had stood in the hall to receive her when she arrived, and when she felt those arms about her, Mary ceased to pine for Inchmahome.

'How you have grown, my daughter!' said the Queen Mother. 'A wonderful future is awaiting you, Mary.'

'Here – in Scotland?'

Her mother shook her head gravely. 'I do not think there would be anything but strife for you here in Scotland,' she said.

'Then I am going away again?'

The Queen Mother nodded. 'To a place very different from Inchmahome.'

'I loved Inchmahome, Mother; I loved the monks.'

'Yes, you were happy there and I believe the time was not ill spent. I trust you worked hard at your French.' The Queen Mother then spoke to Mary in her native language so rapidly that Mary could not understand her.

Her mother clicked her tongue. 'Oh dear, you are not proficient enough. That is a pity. Still there is a little time left to us, we must have more and more lessons. I should not like your grandparents to discover that you could not speak their language.'

'I am going to my grandparents?'

A slow smile of satisfaction spread across the Queen Mother's face. 'You will see your grandparents but you will not live with them.'

'Then where shall I live?'

'At the Court of France,' answered her mother. 'Oh my daughter, that day will be the happiest in my life when you are married to the Dauphin.'

Mary was silent. She had so recently returned; was she to leave her home almost immediately for a land across the sea?

What a bustle there was in the Castle of Stirling! In the schoolroom the dressmakers were busy; in the Queen's apartments her clothes were being packed; and nowadays her mother always spoke to her in French.

She would click her tongue with impatience. 'What are your grandparents going to say! What will the King think! How will you be able to speak to the Dauphin – in an accent which smacks of the Lowlands of Scotland!'

Each morning the five Marys were given a lesson in French by the Queen Mother herself, and they were expected to speak in French even when they were alone together. It was very disturbing and spoilt all the excitement of preparation.

There were occasions when Mary felt rather frightened, because going to France was very different from going to Inchmahome. On the island she had been allowed to run wild when she was not at her lessons; it would be very different in France.

Her mother tried to explain the customs of the French Court.

'We French observe etiquette more strictly than the Scots do. You must quickly learn what is right and what is wrong, and make sure that there are no mistakes.'

'Oh Mother,' cried Mary, 'I do not want to go to France. Not yet. I want to stay here for a while.'

'That is nonsense,' retorted the Queen Mother. 'You should be the happiest girl in the world.'

'But you are not coming with me.'

'Alas, how I wish that I were. But Queens and Princesses have to learn to obey; they have to be prepared to leave their families – even when they are very young. It is the first task of a Queen to remember her duty to her subjects. When you are married to the Dauphin, you will be the wife of the heir to the throne. And when the King of France dies – which we trust will not be for many years – you will be the Queen.'

'But why cannot I rule in Scotland where I am already Queen?'

'Because, my love, it is for Scotland's good that we should unite this country with France. Together we should be strong against the English.'

Mary twirled the glittering necklace about her mother's neck and watched the light catch the stones. 'It is always the English,' she said.

'Alas, yes. It is always the English. Many of them are in Scotland at this moment. They have captured our towns. We could be in acute danger at any moment. That is why you are to leave for France with all speed, and kind King Henry of France has sent ships to take you to France.'

'Where are the ships?'

'They are at Dumbarton, and soon you will be going there. You will be so proud when you see the mighty ships of France, because you will know that the English would be powerless against them.'

'I do not want to leave you, Mother.'

'Ah, but you must be a brave Queen. Perhaps I shall come to France to see you. The King of France is a very kind man and I am sure he will allow me to do so. He has said that he is very happy for you to have your Marys with you. That is the kind of man the King of France is. Mary, you never knew your father. Well, King Henry II of France will be a father to you.'

Mary considered this. It would be wonderful to have a father; she had often envied those who had them, and she had cried almost as bitterly as Flem had when Lord Fleming had been killed at Pinkie Cleugh.

'And you will have the Dauphin and his sister as your playmates,' went on the Queen Mother.

'I have my Marys as my playmates.'

'Mary, I must speak to you about the Dauphin. He is not very strong and it will be necessary for you to be gentle with him.'

'He is sick?'

'No, but he is delicate and cannot play rough games. So you will take care of him, won't you?'

The Queen Mother watched her daughter shrewdly. She was delighted with the effect of those words. Mary was making up her mind that the Dauphin should be her especial care, and because of this her attitude had changed; now she was looking forward to going to France.

Mary had stood on deck for as long as she could see her mother waving the white kerchief which she had carried especially for this purpose.

'Goodbye, my mother. Goodbye, Scotland,' she murmured; and she was momentarily sad because, although she was not very old, she seemed to have said goodbye too often in her life.

How different this from the journey to Inchmahome! How grand was the French ship which was to carry her from Dumbarton to the coast of France!

This ship was full of handsome men with curled beards and excited voices. Mary, her four Marys with her, watching them all, feeling the salt breeze tugging at her hood, could not but feel excited.

Lady Fleming, who was with them, was not very happy because she hated the rise and fall of the ship which so pleased the Marys.

'How I wish we were there!' she wailed. 'I can't wait to be there. These perilous voyages terrify me.'

'You must be brave, Aunt Janet,' Mary told her.

But Lady Fleming turned away and went to her cabin.

What fun it was running about the ship, and how eager the jolly Frenchmen were to answer questions! They laughed at the French of the five Marys; and they told them it was enchanting. That was a very happy journey because Mary realized that everyone was trying to tell her how welcome she would be in her new country.

Of course Lady Fleming was wretched, simply because she was sick and hated the sea. But Mary did her best to comfort her and there was nothing to worry about because Lady Fleming would be quite happy as soon as she set foot on the soil of France.

There was a moment of terror when English ships were sighted on the horizon, and the rumour went through the ship that news had spread below the Border that the Queen of Scots was on her way to France. Orders were given for the crew to be prepared to defend the ship.

The Marys watched these preparations with interested excitement, and when the English ships were lost to sight, and a great cheer went up on deck, they joined in.

Afterwards they played hide-and-seek all over the ship, and the sailors laughed with pleasure to watch them, and were ready to hide the Queen in places where it was impossible for those who sought her to find her.

All too soon there was a sudden shout of: 'Land!' and even Lady Fleming, pale and most unlike her pretty self, came hurrying on deck to see the coast of France.

'I never thought I should live through the ordeal!' she sighed. 'Praise the saints, the danger is almost past.'

And so they came into Roscoff – a little port in Brittany.

It was a triumphant journey that Mary made across her adopted country. The French seemed determined that she should know how pleased they were to have her there, and as soon as she stepped ashore Mary saw the gay banners fluttering in the breeze and was able to read the words on them: *'Vive la Reinette!'* Long live the little Queen!

These words were called to her as she rode through the French towns and villages where the people came out of their houses and lined the roads to see her pass. The French were so much more gay than the people of Scotland and they made no secret of their pleasure. They threw flowers at her; they danced their country dances at the roadside for her pleasure; and they shouted that she was the loveliest little Queen they had ever seen.

When the cavalcade, of which she was the centre, reached the town of Nantes, they found a barge waiting to carry them along the River Loire to Tours where the Queen's grandparents, the great Duke of Guise and his wife the Duchess who before her marriage had been Antoinette de Bourbon, would be waiting to accompany them to the French Court.

On the waters of the Loire they sailed. Mary with her four little friends, watching the country-side; here also the villages were decorated and their inhabitants lined the river banks to shout *'Vive la Reinette!'* Through the luscious vineyards of Anjou and Touraine they went, and the scenery as much as the people delighted Mary.

But as they came nearer to Tours she began to feel a little uneasy, for here she must meet those magnificent grandparents of hers of whom she had heard so much, and she could not enjoy the scenery because she was rehearsing how she would greet them in French.

She must be word perfect; there must be no trace of that

Lowland accent. Mary told the Marys that she wished they could go sailing on and on and need never reach Tours.

But at last they were there, and waiting for her were the great Duke and his wife, every bit as grand and ceremonious as Mary had expected them to be.

Now all their companions had become stiff and guarded. It was as though they said: It was all very well to laugh and joke before, but now we are in the presence of the mighty Duke and his Duchess; now we must remember our dignity and theirs.

As Mary left the ship she saw the Duke and Duchess waiting to receive her. They did not greet her as though they were her grandparents; the Duke bowed and the Duchess curtseyed, for, strange as it seemed, although she was so much in awe of them, Mary was a Queen and they merely a Duke and Duchess.

Mary felt ashamed that they should bow to her, and she smiled at them disarmingly; but that, it seemed, was the wrong thing to do, for both grandparents regarded her with solemn speculation.

'Apartments have been prepared for Your Majesty,' said the Duchess, 'and I shall conduct you to them without delay.'

Mary thanked her rather shakily in an accent which was not really her best, and she fancied she saw a frown appear on her grandmother's brow.

But as soon as they were alone, her grandmother's attitude changed completely; she threw aside all restraint, and sitting down she took Mary on to her lap and kissed her tenderly.

The Duke came in and stood smiling in a very kindly way at Mary, so that she felt she had not understood her grandparents at all on their first meeting.

'We are very pleased with our granddaughter,' said the Duchess.

'Her mother's reports did not lie,' added the Duke, and Mary was relieved because she saw that he was as delighted with her as her grandmother was.

'I thought I had displeased you,' she told them. 'You seemed so cold.'

'Ah, that was necessary for the sake of etiquette. It is one of the greatest sins at the Court of France to ignore etiquette. Therfore when we meet you in public it is the Duke and Duchess of Guise meeting the Queen of Scots; but in private it is Grandpapa, Grandmama and their granddaughter.'

This made Mary laugh with happiness. 'Everything that happens in France is wonderful,' she told them.

'Ah,' said the Duchess smiling at the Duke, 'I can see our granddaughter is going to be a credit to us. I shall write to Francis at once and tell him of our pleasure.'

'Is that my Uncle Francis?' Mary asked.

'It is, my child.'

'My mother said he was the greatest soldier in France.'

'She spoke the truth. Francis, who is the Duke of Aumale, was born to be a leader. So was your Uncle Charles, Francis's brother, who is the Cardinal of Lorraine. You will meet them both all in good time, and they will tell you what you must do. If you need any advice at any time you must go to Uncle Francis or Uncle Charles, or come to us. It is a rule of the family that the Guises all stand together; and never forget, Mary, that you are a Guise.'

'No, I never shall. My mother has always said that I must remember it.'

Her grandmother kissed her forehead, still smiling.

'Now, my dear, you will wish to hear what plans are being made for you. I shall come with you to Carrières where the royal children are now staying. It is not far from the Palace of Saint-Germain.'

'Are the King and Queen there too?'

'No. The Court is at Moulins. It has left Saint-Germain while the palace is being sweetened. We are fastidious here in France and do not live too long in one place, but after a few months move on so that everything may be made clean and sweet. I understand that manners in Scotland are a little rough. Never mind, you will soon learn the ways of the French. I shall take you to the nurseries myself. I have heard that the Dauphin can scarcely wait to see you.'

'I look forward to seeing him too.'

'It will be a very pleasant journey and you will see how eagerly the people welcome you in every town through which you pass. We shall go by river to Orléans and then on by road.'

'I hope the Dauphin likes my Marys.'

A shadow crossed the Duchess's face.

'I am sure he will – in time.'

'In time?' repeated Mary blankly.

'Well, my dear, the King is very anxious for you and the Dauphin to be the best of friends, and he feels that just at first you should be alone with him.' Noticing the dismay in Mary's face the Duchess hurried on: 'It is only for a week or so. He has ordered that the Marys shall not accompany you to Carrières but shall join you later.'

'But we are always together,' stammered Mary, and she could not prevent her lower lip's trembling.

'The company of the Dauphin will compensate you for the loss of them during the next few weeks,' said the Duchess complacently. 'After all, he is the son of the King of France.'

'They are not to be sent back to England?' said Mary suspiciously.

'Oh no, no. I can promise you that.'

But the Duchess's assurances could not console her, and for the first time since her arrival in France Mary felt uneasy.

5

The Royal Family of France

In the company of her grandmother and certain of the latter's attendants, Mary entered the nurseries at Carrières.

The first person she noticed was the boy who was standing uncertainly with a tall man and woman. He looked very hesitant, that little boy. Little he certainly was, being shorter than Mary; and because his head seemed over-large for his body he seemed still smaller. His legs and arms were very thin and his face pale. He gave the impression that what he wanted to do more than anything was turn from the newcomers and go and hide himself somewhere.

The Duchess spoke first. 'Ah, Monsieur le Maréchal, I bring my granddaughter, the Queen of Scotland, to Carrières.' She went forward then and curtseyed to the little boy who gave a nervous smile.

'Madame,' went on the Duchess now addressing the lady, 'it is the King's express command that on this occasion we dispense with ceremony. He wants the meeting between the children to be as informal as possible.'

'I know those to be His Majesty's orders,' said the lady.

Mary, who had been watching the boy all this time, at last caught his eye and smiled at him in a friendly fashion. The boy immediately returned the smile, but very shyly.

Then Mary saw the little girl; she was pretty but looked very frail, and Mary realized at once that both the royal children lacked her good health. That made her sorry for them and she remembered what her mother had told her about taking care of the Dauphin.

Of course, that was what she would do. She would look after him, make him less shy, make him realize that, although he was a little boy, he was the son of the King and had no need to feel frightened of anyone.

Without thinking she went to the Dauphin and, taking him in her arms, kissed him. He looked somewhat startled; so did the others; but her grandmother lifted a finger and whispered: 'This is as it should be. A spontaneous greeting. How I wish His Majesty were here to see these charming children together.'

Mary did not hear them; nor did the Dauphin; they were so absorbed in each other.

'I am Mary,' she told him. 'I have come to be your friend and playmate.'

'I – I know of you,' stammered the boy.

She nodded. 'We have to love each other,' said Mary. Then she smiled: 'That will be very easy.'

The Dauphin smiled slowly and a faint flush touched his

pale cheeks. 'Yes, Mary,' he said, 'that will be very easy.'

The Duchess then said: 'That is a good beginning. Now, this is the Governor of the royal nursery, the Maréchal d'Humières and Madame d'Humières. Ah, and here is Madame Elisabeth.'

The little girl came forward and curtseyed to Mary – for although she was a Princess of France, Mary was a Queen, and even at her age she understood enough of the etiquette of the Court to know what was expected of her.

But Mary spontaneously embraced her as she had her brother, for it seemed to her that the girl was in as much need of her friendship as the Dauphin was.

'I shall love you as I shall love the Dauphin,' Mary told her, and Elisabeth threw her arms about Mary and kissed her fervently.

'How did you come here?' asked the Dauphin, who clearly did not want his sister to take all Mary's attention.

'In a big ship,' Mary answered.

'What sort of ship?'

As Mary began to describe the ship she saw that the grown-ups were quietly leaving the apartment, which rather pleased her for she felt it was so much easier to get to know her new friends without their supervision.

She immediately took charge, as she did with the Marys, and said: 'Let us go and sit in the window and I will tell you all about myself and you shall tell me all about yourselves.'

The Dauphin and his sister listened intently to all she said, and she knew that it was none the less interesting because her accent was a little strange to them. She told them of her four Marys who would soon be with them; she chattered away, lapsing now and then into English. So much had happened to her, so little to them, that they thought she was wonderful.

How exciting it seemed to have ridden through the night, not knowing whither she was bound, and to wake up in the monastery of Inchmahome! How they enjoyed hearing of

life in the monastery and of Brother Aloysius's herb garden!
Suddenly the Dauphin put his arm through hers and
cried: 'Mary, you must stay with us always. You must promise never, never to leave us.'

So after all Mary did not miss the four Marys as much as she
believed she would. It was two weeks since she had come to
Carrières, and she spent the whole of the days in the
company of Francis, the Dauphin, and his little sister
Elisabeth.

The French children could not bear to be separated from
her, and Mary was very happy in their company, for they
both admired her so much and Mary liked to be admired.
Moreover she was a natural leader, and the Dauphin and his
sister were only too ready to follow her in everything. She
was the one who arranged which games they should play –
and she chose the leading part in them. Francis and Elisabeth did not mind this in the least; in fact they expected it.
Although only a few weeks older than the Dauphin, she
seemed by far the senior; she was so much more healthy, so
much taller, so much more experienced. She taught them
the games she had played with the Marys; hide-and-seek
was a great favourite; they played games of make-believe,
and pretended that they were in the monastery of Inchmahome and that the four Marys were with them.

The Dauphin and his sister had never imagined a playmate so wonderful as Mary, and even in two short weeks
they became much bolder, a little more noisy, more as
normal healthy children should be. So said the Duchess of
Guise who took great pleasure in visiting the royal nursery
to see how the friendship between her granddaughter and
the heir to the throne was progressing.

One day, when Mary had arranged a game of hide-and-
seek, the door of the nursery was suddenly thrown open.
Mary, who was to be the seeker and was sitting at the table,
her head buried in her hands while she counted up to
twenty, peeped through her fingers and saw a very tall man

dressed in black velvet who had a black beard streaked with white. She noticed his kind expression at once as he smiled and cried: 'Where is the Dauphin?'

Francis, who had been hiding behind the tapestry, gave a cry of joy and ran out into the room. He threw himself at the man, who picked him up and held him high over his head.

Little Elisabeth also came running from her hiding-place. She went straight to this man and stood waiting for him to give some of his attention to her.

'So you are glad to see your Papa,' said the man in a deep rumbling voice. 'But I understood you had a new play-fellow.'

'It is Mary!' said the Dauphin.

As Mary rose from the table she felt a wave of excitement because she had guessed from the conversation that this man was the King of France.

She went towards him and knelt before him.

He had put down the Dauphin and his fingers caressed the top of Elisabeth's head as he said: 'Rise, my little one. So you are the Queen of the Scots.'

'Yes, Sire,' answered Mary.

He smiled and Mary was happy because here in France was another person whom she could love. Here was the father whom she had missed all her life until this moment.

Several people had come into the room; and the King turned to them and said: 'My friends, this is my new daughter. I know I am going to be well pleased with her.'

Then one by one all those present come forward and knelt before Mary, taking her hand and kissing it in the French fashion while she stood still and stately, as her mother had taught her.

Francis, Elisabeth and their father stood by, looking on in admiration. And the King whispered to those who stood close to him: 'This is the most beautiful and charming child I ever saw.'

A chair was brought in and the King sat in it, and as he

did so he told his attendants that he wanted to be alone with the children.

When the others were gone he said: 'There, now we are alone and we can forget that we are a King, Queen, Dauphin and Princess. We will merely be ourselves, eh?'

He drew Mary to him and the Dauphin and his sister leaned against their father's knee; and the very way they did so told Mary how much they loved him. The Dauphin was no longer shy; he began to chatter about what Mary had told them and what games they played since she had come.

'And you have become fast friends, I am sure,' said the King.

'We will never, never leave each other,' said Francis.

'And you, Mary, how do you feel about this friendship?'

'I never want to leave Francis either,' she told the King, 'because I am going to make him big and strong.'

'How will you do this?' the King asked.

'By making him not afraid.'

'By making him as you are. Is that so?'

'Well, I might be afraid of something, but then I am young yet.'

The King laughed and touched her cheek with his finger. 'Mary,' he said, 'I want you to make the Dauphin and his sister as merry as you are. Will you do that for me?'

'It is what I have come here to do,' she answered. 'That, and to be your daughter. I always wanted a father; and I only had one for a little while when I was such a baby that I didn't know he was there. So I am very happy to have you for a father.'

'Because you know I am the King of France?'

Mary shook her head. She stood on tiptoe to kiss the edge of the black and silver beard. 'Not only that,' she said. 'But because you are good and kind and what I have always wanted for a father.'

The King wondered whether she had been taught to say just that by her grandparents who, he knew, were two of the most ambitious people in France. Even so, he thought, she says it very charmingly; and I could not find a child whom I would rather see in my children's nurseries.

He was delighted with the change in Francis and Elisabeth, for he had been a little anxious about them because previously they had seemed listless and had never known how to amuse themselves.

'So,' he said, 'you are glad you have come to France.'

'Yes, but I had to say goodbye to my mother.'

'It may well be that we can arrange for her to come and see you here.'

'She has to govern my kingdom while I am away, but I do not think that I need be parted from my friends.'

'What friends are these?'

'My Marys. They came to France with me. They are in France – not very far away – but they are not allowed to come to me here.'

She was looking at the King pleadingly; she was asking that she need no longer be separated from Beaton, Seton, Livy and Flem; and suddenly she felt a wave of exultation sweep over her. She knew that the separation was over, for she was asking her new father that it should be so, and he was all-powerful and would grant her request. He was that sort of father.

It was indeed a happy day when the four Marys came to Carrières.

Mary was hilariously gay. She could not wait to show them to the Dauphin; as for Francis and his sister, they were just as eager to see the Marys, and to welcome them, because they wished to do everything to please *their* Mary.

The nursery was full of the shrill voices while Mary told them of what had been happening to her since their separation, and they told Mary what had happened to them. But eventually they wondered what they were going to do, and Mary said they would show the Dauphin and his sister how to dance a Scottish reel.

This they did to the great delight of the French children; and when they had finished Mary said they should all dance.

The French children had not yet been taught how to dance, and they were too shy to try, but Mary insisted.

'If I had my lute,' said Mary, 'I would play.'

'But if you played for us, you would not be able to dance,' the Dauphin pointed out. 'And I would dance with no one but you.'

'Then we will sing as we dance,' announced Mary; and this they did.

The Dauphin was clumsy but very eager to learn. Seton took little Elisabeth as her partner, and Flem took Livy, while Beaton capered about them as they taught the French children the dancing steps.

There was so much noise that they did not hear the door open, and Mary, looking up suddenly, was startled to see a woman standing in the doorway watching them.

As Mary stared at this woman she felt a shiver run down her spine, for it seemed to her that there was something evil in that pale, flat face which looked neither angry nor pleased. Now everyone else in the room was aware of the intruder's presence. The four Marys stood very still waiting for the Queen to say something. As for the Dauphin and his sister, they seemed fascinated by that figure in the doorway rather in the manner that rabbits might be in the presence of a stoat.

Mary was impulsive and often acted without thinking.

Because something in this woman frightened her a little she was angry with her; the woman had interrupted their dance; they had been having such fun a moment before and now she had come in and spoilt it. Mary saw that the woman was simply dressed in dark colours and that she wore no jewels; she therefore guessed her to be someone in a minor position at the Court. In which case, thought Mary, it was impertinent of her to come unannounced into the room.

'How dare you intrude in this fashion?' said Mary haughtily.

The woman laughed; it was a horrible laugh; deep and rumbling, it shook her plump body so that her cheeks looked like jelly. She seemed very amused.

'Must I ask your permission to come to the nursery?' she said. 'This is something I have to learn.'

'You are impertinent,' retorted Mary and, because she saw that the Dauphin had turned very pale – which indicated that he was afraid – and because she was determined to protect him, and wanted to show him how bold she could be, she drew herself to her full height and went on: 'I should like to remind you that you are speaking to the Queen of Scotland.'

Again that evil laugh rang out. Then the words came, and they filled Mary with apprehension. 'I must inform you,' said the woman, 'that you are speaking to the Queen of France.'

Mary gasped. She looked at the Dauphin for confirmation, but he seemed to have shrunk to half his size while little Elisabeth had crept closer to Mary as though begging her to protect her.

Mary stammered: 'The Queen – of France? But that is impossible.'

'Do you think so?' The woman had come closer. 'Come, my son,' she said, holding out a hand to the shrinking Dauphin, 'come and pay homage to the Queen of France as a good son should.'

The Dauphin went to his mother and knelt before her. 'You are flushed,' she said. 'Overheated by these rough games, eh? It would seem we have a little barbarian in our nurseries. We must watch that she does not influence you with her rough manners.'

The Dauphin rose and stood aside for Elisabeth to kneel before her mother.

The Queen of France was waiting for Mary to pay her similar homage, and there was nothing Mary, scarlet with embarrassment, could do but kneel before her.

Then Mary knew; this was the Italian Woman (as she was often called) Catherine de' Medici, who had married Henry II of France, and who was disliked and distrusted throughout the land, but who was nevertheless Queen of France.

Mary rose to her feet and looked into that bland, smiling face.

She had found many to love in France, but here was one who would most certainly be her enemy.

6

The Battle of the Queens

After that unfortunate meeting with the Queen of France,
Mary expected some trouble from that quarter. None came
in the following weeks; but every time she was in the presence of Queen Catherine, she would feel afraid and she
could not prevent her eyes straying to that plump, black-clad
figure, when always the expressionless eyes would be fixed
on her and a smile would appear on the flat face. It was an
alarming smile for there was no friendliness in it; Mary
thought it sly and cunning and wondered what lay behind
it.

Sometimes Queen Catherine would come into the nursery so silently that they would not hear her until she was there; it sent a shiver down Mary's spine to look up suddenly and see those eyes upon her. Games lost all their spontaneous fun when Mary knew that Queen Catherine was at Carrières.

But to be at the French Court was a very exciting experience. The magnificence of the royal apartments delighted Mary who quickly developed a taste for beautiful clothes and furniture. This was very different from the Castle of Stirling. But in a few days Mary ceased to marvel and forgot that she had ever lived in the frugal Court of Scotland, and felt as though she had always known the luxury of France.

Her uncle, the Duke of Aumale was to be married, and this was a very grand occasion because all the most noble men and women in the land would assemble for it.

A few days before the ceremony Mary was being dressed by her attendants, with Lady Fleming in charge, when news was brought to her that her uncles had arrived and were asking to see her.

Mary was delighted; this was a pleasure to which she had looked forward so long. In the old days in Scotland she had pictured Uncle Francis and Uncle Charles as men like gods. Her mother had impressed upon her that they were the most influential men in France. Always it had been: 'You must not do this, or that. What would your uncles think if they knew!'

And at last she was to come face to face with them. But a certain apprehension modified her excitement. What would they think of her?

She was inclined to believe that since she had come to France she had been a little spoiled – except of course by Queen Catherine. Would her mother think she had perhaps become a little vain, a little too eager for pleasure?

So, it was with some uncertainty that she went to her uncles' apartment.

There they stood, waiting for her, and as she paused on

the threshold of the room she felt the blood rush to her cheeks for they looked exactly as she had pictured them. Uncle Francis de Guise, the Duke of Aumale, was indeed like a god. He was tall, the handsomest man she had seen in France – for although he was so good-looking he lacked what she had come to think of as prettiness, which was a feature of so many of the men she saw. Uncle Francis was every inch a soldier. He had a wonderful, curly black beard and brilliant dark eyes, strong features, tanned complexion, and in his uniform he was a startling figure.

And beside him was Uncle Charles in the red robes of a Cardinal, tall and as handsome in his way as Uncle Francis was in his. He lacked Francis's ruddy looks for he was pale, but in fact his features were more clear-cut and he reminded Mary of a Greek statue she had seen.

'So here is our little niece,' said Uncle Francis, whose voice was loud; and he spoke like a soldier.

Then Uncle Charles: 'For so long we have awaited this pleasure.' His voice was like music, soft, gentle, yet somehow full of meaning.

Mary went forward and curtseyed.

Uncle Francis lifted her in his arms and kissed her heartily on both cheeks. Then it was Uncle Charles's turn. She smelt the delicious scent which came from his clothes when he kissed her as Uncle Francis had done. He did not release her but drew her close to him; she liked the soft silk of his red robes and again she smelled that delicious scent.

'We hear good reports of you,' said Uncle Francis.

'I am glad, for I do not think the Queeen likes me.'

'The Queen!' The uncles exchanged glances. 'We shall not allow the Italian Woman to disturb the Guises, my child. She is of no importance.'

Mary sighed with relief. 'I feared she might be, since she is Queen.'

'Do not give her a thought,' said Uncle Charles. He sat down and took her on to his knee. He lifted her curls admiringly. 'Is she not a pretty creature?' he asked his brother.

'I had heard reports of her beauty, but even so I am most agreeably surprised.'

Mary dimpled with pleasure, and even as she did so thought: My mother would not be pleased, for I am becoming very vain.

Her uncles however did not seem to mind this vanity; on the other hand, it amused them.

'We have heard with great satisfaction,' said Uncle Francis, 'that the Dauphin is your slave.'

'And if,' added Uncle Charles, 'you are a clever little girl, as I am sure you are, you will keep him so. Then in a few years' time you must persuade him that two such fond companions should without delay become husband and wife.'

Mary opened her eyes wide and looked from one uncle to the other. They were wise men and she was only an inexperienced little girl, but she sensed deep meaning behind their words.

'Oh, we shall have to wait until we are fifteen or sixteen for that,' she said.

'It may not be necessary to wait so long,' murmured Uncle Charles.

'But people don't marry before they are that age.'

'You, my little Mary,' said Uncle Charles in a very tender voice, 'are not people. You are the Queen of Scots and above all you are the niece of the Duke of Aumale and the Cardinal of Lorraine. The Duke of Guise is your grandfather. Your uncle and I will be very happy when we see our niece Dauphine of France.'

'And,' said Mary shrewdly, 'you want that so much that you do not want to wait too long for it.'

Her uncles laughed and told her she was a clever girl, and they were sure that she would be a credit to her family, the powerful Guises. They gave her sweetmeats and she sang and played on the lute for them. When she had left them, her two uncles talked of Mary.

'As soon as possible that marriage must take place,' said Francis. 'What if the Dauphin should die before it is celebrated? The boy is very delicate and I don't feel he'll make old bones.'

'All our plans would come to nothing,' Charles answered. 'Oh yes, that marriage must not be delayed a day longer than we can help. Then it will only remain for the King to die and our Mary will be Queen of France. And through our lovely niece, brother, we shall rule this land.'

Mary's first ball at the Court of France was that given to celebrate the marriage of her Uncle Francis to Anne d'Este, the daughter of the Duke of Ferrara. The bride was beautiful and the bridegroom surely the most handsome man in France, yet at that ball it was the Queen of Scots who was the centre of attraction.

For Mary had insisted that the Dauphin dance with her, and young Francis, shy as he was, could refuse Mary nothing. So he had agreed to learn to dance; they had practised often together and when they went into the centre of the *salle de bal*, the King signed for everyone else to leave the floor so that he might watch his son and his betrothed.

Mary was so lovely in her gown of blue velvet with her tartan sash held in place by the agraffe, her lovely hair falling over her shoulders, that those present could not take their eyes from her; and even young Francis, dancing with her, appeared to dance well.

The King was delighted, for the Dauphin had never danced in public before, and with the colour in his cheeks he looked almost healthy.

The bridegroom, who was standing by the King's chair, whispered: 'And what does Your Majesty think of our little niece?'

'I am enchanted with her,' answered the King.

Mary could have been completely happy if there had been no Queen Catherine, as there always seemed to be some excitement going on at the French Court. Lessons had to be done, it was true, but Mary enjoyed lessons, particularly as she was so far in advance of her companions. Her grandmother, the Duchess of Guise, together with Uncle Charles, arranged her time-table; the Marys always shared her lessons, and sometimes the Dauphin and Elisabeth did also.

One of the most important occasions at that time was the coronation of Queen Catherine. The King had already been crowned, and now it was Queen Catherine's turn. Mary had at first refused to be excited about this event, because Queen Catherine was to be the centre of it, but eventually she was caught up in the general bustle.

'What fun it would be,' she said to Lady Fleming, 'if Catherine were not the Queen, but someone else was – someone kind and beautiful, worthy of my dear father.'

She had taken to calling the King Papa as the Dauphin and Elisabeth did, and he was delighted that she should do so; she would never call Catherine Mama. 'Nothing would induce me to do that!' she declared.

But she did enjoy the coronation very much. The pageantry was such as she had never seen before in the whole of her life, and exceeded that of her uncle's wedding. She had to admit, though reluctantly, that even the Queen looked beautiful on that day. As for the King, dressed in silver lace riding under a blue velvet canopy on which were embroidered the golden lilies of France – he was a father to be proud of.

It was shortly after the coronation that Queen Catherine paid one of her stealthy visits to the schoolroom where the five Marys were working with the Dauphin and Elisabeth.

Lady Fleming sat at the head of the table supervising their lessons.

When Lady Fleming was in charge there was usually a great deal of chatter and hilarity, and as the door was opened, there was so much laughter at the table that no one heard it.

Then suddenly Lady Fleming looked up and the laughter froze on her face; Mary knew, even before she saw who had come in, that Queen Catherine was watching them.

There was immediate silence at the table as Queen Catherine came forward. Lady Fleming stumbled to her feet and made a low curtsey, but Queen Catherine scarcely looked at her; her eyes were on the children who rose and made their bow or curtsey.

The Queen laughed in that unpleasant way of hers which was more of a sneer than a laugh. With her was one of her women who was not unlike her and whom the children had often seen in her company.

'Pray be seated, all of you,' she cried, and as they immediately obeyed she went on: 'How amusing lessons seem to have become since the Queen of Scotland joined our nursery.' She glanced briefly at Lady Fleming. 'I have come to see how the *lessons* progress; I know how the merrymaking does.'

She sat down at the table in between the Dauphin and Mary and laid her plump white hand on the paper on which Mary had been writing.

Francis sat very still, and Mary knew that he was terrified because the Queen sat between them.

'Ha,' said the Queen, looking at the Dauphin's work, 'you will have to work harder if you would be a scholar, eh, my son?'

'Yes, Your Majesty.'

Now she had drawn Mary's work towards her. It was a Latin exercise, and smiling she took up a pen and underlined a mistake she had discovered.

'And we constantly hear how clever the Queen of Scots is,' she whispered. She took Mary's ear between her thumb and finger and pinched it, just hard enough to hurt. Mary gasped and the Queen laughed and she released Mary's ear and pushed her work towards her. 'It seems that the Queen of Scots can make mistakes,' she added as she rose.

'Lady Fleming,' she went on, 'I fear you are over-worked. You need help in this task. I shall suggest that you be relieved of certain of your duties.' She turned to the woman who had come with her into the schoolroom. 'Madame de Paroy,' she went on, 'I am sure that you would make an excellent governess for this merry little brood.'

Mary, who had not yet learned to restrain herself, said quickly: 'Lady Fleming has always been my governess. I am well pleased with her.'

The Queen gave her a look of mock consideration. 'Is that so?' she remarked. Then she was staring at Mary's exercise with the correction on it. 'Well, we shall see,' she murmured.

When she left the apartment, there was silence for a few seconds, then Mary burst out: 'I shall not allow it. I shall speak to the King. I know he will not allow that woman to come here if I ask him.'

She looked at the Dauphin who was white with fear; as for little Elisabeth, she was still trembling.

The four Marys looked cowed – even Beaton. This was the effect Queen Catherine had on them all.

Mary did not see the King until the following day and then, to her chagrin when he came to visit the schoolroom, Queen Catherine was with him. And in attendance on the Queen was the odious Madame de Paroy.

Mary however had sworn to Francis and Elisabeth, as well as the four Marys, that the next time she saw the King she would plead with him not to send Madame de Paroy to look after them, and she knew that she must keep her promise.

Catherine began in her sly way by commending Lady Fleming on her care of the children. 'It is a great task and I fear it is too much for you.'

'I assure Your Majesty,' answered Lady Fleming, 'that it is a task of the utmost enjoyment. It does not tire me in the least.'

'Nevertheless I feel you need help.'

Mary went to the King and took his hand. He smiled down at her with the affection he always bestowed upon her.

'Papa, may I make a request?' she asked.

'Of course, my child.'

'Please do not allow Madame de Paroy to be our governess.'

The King looked at the Queen, who returned the look with a smile and a slight lifting of her shoulders as though to say, What strange notions children get!

'Her Majesty the Queen is eager not to tax Lady Fleming's strength too far,' he said to Mary. 'It is for this reason that she suggested Madame de Paroy should share her duty.'

'We do not want Madame de Paroy in the nursery,' retorted Mary bluntly.

Catherine gave her sudden hard laugh in which Madame de Paroy joined.

Mary turned to look at the Dauphin who immediately ran to his father and said:

'Oh please do not send Madame de Paroy here, please, Papa, please.'

'Why do you not want her, my son?' the King asked.

The Dauphin said promptly: 'Because Mary does not.'

Catherine seemed unable to suppress her mirth.

'When we put a Queen in our nursery,' she said meaningly, 'we must expect her to rule.'

'And my little Elisabeth?' asked the King, turning to his daughter, 'what does she wish?'

'I do not want Madame de Paroy to come here,' Elisabeth promptly replied.

Catherine caught her daughter's arm and Mary noticed the girl winced as she did so. 'Because Mary does not, eh?'

'Y – yes—' stammered Elisabeth.

The King smiled at the Queen. 'It would seem matters should remain as they are.'

Catherine turned to Lady Fleming and smiled as though she were her friend. 'I am sorry,' she said. 'I thought only to help you.'

When the grown-ups had left the nursery, Mary seized the Dauphin and began to dance round the room with him.

'We've won! We've won!' she cried; and she was secretly telling herself that there was nothing to fear from the Queen Catherine.

The Dauphin and Elisabeth had retired to their own apartments, and the five Marys were with Lady Fleming in the schoolroom.

Now that the French children were absent it was easier to be frank, because Mary felt that, odious as Queen Catherine was, she was still the mother of Francis and Elisabeth and it was not possible to discuss her freely in their presence.

Lady Fleming, now that she was no longer under the eye of Mary's mother, was becoming more and more indiscreet, and it often seemed to Mary that she was like an older sister rather than a governess. This was an endearing quality, of course, and Mary would not have had it otherwise. She shuddered to think what the friendly, easy-going nursery would be like with the stern Madame de Paroy in charge.

'It is clear,' Lady Fleming was saying now, 'that the Queen has no influence with the King. I couldn't help laughing to see how ready he was to do what you wanted.'

'Oh,' replied Mary blithely, 'he always wants to please me.'

'Yet she is his Queen!' cried Beaton.

'He was forced to marry her,' put in Flem. 'He would never have done so from choice.'

'I should say not!' declared Lady Fleming. 'Poor dear man. They are not suited to each other.'

'Who would be suited to her but a – a snake!' demanded Mary; and they all laughed.

T–C

'I am only sorry,' Mary went on, 'that when I marry Francis *she* will be my mother-in-law. That spoils what might be perfection. Imagine me, a Queen of Scotland, having as my mother-in-law a woman who has no breeding, who is vulgar! How I wish she would go home to her own family of Italian merchants.'

Mary felt Seton's warning eyes upon her, and looking up saw what she had seen on other occasions. The door had quietly opened and Catherine was standing silently on the threshold of the room.

The question was, how long had she been standing there? How much had she heard? Certainly she would have heard that last sentence of Mary's.

I don't care! thought Mary defiantly. It's true.

Now that she was discovered, Catherine advanced into the room. 'Merry as ever,' she said with her laugh. 'I came to speak to the Dauphin, but I see that he has already retired.'

Then, giving them all her slow, sly smile, she went out.

There was a silence in the schoolroom. They were all asking themselves how much she could have heard.

She will hate me more than ever, thought Mary. And I don't care. I simply don't care.

There was consternation at the Court.

Mary had had a slight chill and been confined to her bed; special gruel had been sent up to her, yet she had not taken it, but given it to one of her pages who, after eating it, had been violently ill.

The inference seemed obvious: Someone had tried to poison the Queen of Scots.

The King was dismayed. He had all her servants questioned, as well as all those who had been anywhere near her.

He asked that neither Mary nor any of the children should be told of this matter, because he did not wish them to be alarmed. Meanwhile the questioning went on and at length an archer of the Scottish guard, who had come to France with Mary, confessed that he had poisoned the gruel.

He was imprisoned and put to the question, but he would say no more; he was punished with death, but the mystery of who had bribed him to do this remained unsolved.

Queen Catherine talked to the King of the matter.

She said: 'There must be no more attempts on the Queen's life, and it seems to me that, had those whose duty it is to watch over her been more watchful, this would never have happened. Lady Fleming is a frivolous creature, more given to flirtation and gaiety than the care of children. She serves little purpose here. I think she should be sent back to Scotland. Madame de Paroy would make a more reliable governess.'

'The children did not appear to want Madame de Paroy.'

The Queen puffed with her lips – a habit of hers which Mary had always hated as much as that sudden loud laugh. 'Mary does not want her. Therefore the others do not. Really, our son should think for himself. He should not be put into leading strings by this girl from Scotland. It is pleasant enough to know that they are fond of each other, but he must assert himself sometimes. No, our Francis and Elisabeth would be happy enough with Madame de Paroy; and so would Mary after a while. You must agree that Lady Fleming has proved she is not the right governess for the children.'

The King was thoughful; there was a great deal in what the Queen said, he had to admit.

The King had left Saint-Germain to make a ceremonial tour through his towns, that he might have an opportunity of showing himself to his subjects. With him went his friends and courtiers, but he considered that the Dauphin was as yet too young – and not really strong enough – to accompany the Court on such a strenuous journey.

The Queen did not go with him either. This was not an

unusual state of affairs, for the King was glad now and then to escape from his wife's company; as for the rest of the Court they had never really accepted the Italian Woman as one of them; so Catherine stayed behind at Saint-Germain.

Mary was distressed when she realized what was happening. It was bad enough to have to say goodbye to the King – although only temporarily – but to know that the Queen was to remain behind was really disturbing.

Naturally enough with the King away, the Queen was in command; and Saint-Germain was a very different place under the domination of Queen Catherine.

The day after the departure of the King and his Court, Mary went to Lady Fleming's apartment and found her governess lying on her bed, her face hidden among the pillows.

'Aunt Janet!' she cried. 'What is wrong?'

There was no answer, but Mary saw that her governess's shoulders were heaving and that she was crying bitterly. It was always rather disconcerting to see a grown-up in tears, and Mary knelt on the bed and implored Lady Fleming to tell her what had happened.

A face that was ravaged with grief was lifted from the pillows.

'This is her revenge,' stammered Lady Fleming.

There was no need to ask whose. Mary blurted out: 'What has she done?'

'I am to go back to Scotland. I have had my orders.'

'But she cannot do this.'

'She can. The King has given her authority to rule in his absence. She says I have proved myself unfit. I am to leave ... at once. Oh, my dearest, is there nothing we can do?'

'There must be something. I shall never allow it.'

Lady Fleming only shook her head and burst into fresh weeping.

Mary resolutely climbed off the bed.

'Where are you going?' asked Lady Fleming in alarm. But Mary did not wait to answer her; she ran as fast as she could to Queen Catherine's apartment.

The Queen was with some of her women, who did their best to restrain Mary, but she would not allow this and pushed them aside. 'I wish to see the Queen,' she said. 'I demand to see the Queen.'

And there was Catherine, standing before her, smiling her evil smile, knowing full well why Mary had come to her apartment.

'These are my apartments,' she quietly reminded her visitor, and added with sarcasm: 'Even the Queen of Scotland may not give orders here.'

'Madame,' said Mary haughtily, 'my governess, Lady Fleming, is very distressed.'

'Oh,' interrupted Catherine, 'but Lady Fleming is not your governess now, is she?'

'She is. She always has been and I will have no other.'

'In a few days,' Catherine said quietly, 'Lady Fleming is returning to Scotland.'

'I shall not allow that to happen.'

'Alas,' said Catherine, 'you will be unable to prevent it.'

'I tell you that she has always been my governess.'

'And I tell you that she is so no longer.'

'I shall appeal to the King.'

'The King has left me in command, and appointed me your guardian in his absence. Shall we try to be sensible? Lady Fleming is found to be unfit to have the guardianship of my son's future wife. It is as simple as that.'

Looking into that implacable face, Mary realized that she was powerless against the woman. But she did not abandon hope; she fell to her knees and looked up imploringly at the cool smiling face.

'Please – please, Madame, I love Lady Fleming. She has been with me since I was a baby. I am parted from my mother, and she has been as a mother to me.'

'You poor child,' said the Queen, 'to be left to the care of

such an unworthy creature. Have no fear. You call the King
your father, do you not? Then, as I am the King's wife and
mother of the Dauphin, I must be your mother too. So you
see you should not mourn the loss of this Fleming woman,
should you?'

'Please – please,' pleaded Mary.

'You waste your time, my dear. Come, get up. Go back to
your nursery. Call your companions together. I will send
your new governess to you. Then you will see how I have
your welfare at heart.'

Mary knew it was useless to plead. She rose and stumbled
from the room.

They were gathered in the nursery, waiting. Soon their new
governess would come to them. The Dauphin and Elisabeth
were silent and even Mary could not make them smile. The
four Marys waited for a cue from their Queen. Poor Flem
was heartbroken because she had not only said goodbye to a
governess but to her mother.

Queen Catherine came into the room. She was alone. As
she approached the group, the Dauphin bowed and each of
the girls sank to the floor in curtsey.

Catherine stood smiling at them.

'Ah,' she said, 'I see you are all eager to meet your new
governess.' She turned to the door. 'Come in,' she cried. 'The
children are waiting to welcome you.'

And into the schoolroom came the hated Madame de
Paroy.

'My dears,' said Catherine in her cosiest voice, 'here is your
new governess.'

Seven pairs of eyes regarded the new governess with dislike.

'Now,' said Queen Catherine, 'you should show your
pleasure.' She turned to Madame de Paroy. 'The Queen of
Scots regards herself as the leader of this little band. She will
tell us how pleased they all are.'

Mary was silent; she knew the others would take their cue

from her; she kept saying to herself: 'I won't have her in my nursery. I won't. I won't.'

'Come along,' insisted Catherine, gripping Mary's arm so hard that it hurt as her fingers pinched the soft flesh; but although Mary wanted to cry out she set her lips firmly.

'The Queen of Scotland is of an obstinate nature,' Catherine said to Madame de Paroy.

'I see that is so, Madame,' answered the new governess.

'As you know,' went on Catherine, 'I do not wish the children to be beaten unless it is necessary. But I was always one to believe that to spare the rod was to spoil the child.'

Oh, how dare she! though Mary. Does she forget who I am? I shall speak to the King – to my grandmother – to my uncles.

'Great pride is a sin. The whip is good for beating it out of your bodies. As you know, I have had to beat my own children.'

Mary looked at the Dauphin and Elisabeth, and saw that they were trembling.

'So, Madame de Paroy, if you should find obstinacy, pride, stupidity – or any such sins in these young people, I look to you to beat it out of them.'

'Yes, Madame,' said Madame de Paroy.

'I believe you have several canes for the purpose?'

'I have, Madame.'

'Then use them – should it be necessary. Now, Mary, I have asked you to welcome your new governess. Will you do so, or—?'

The fingers pinching Mary's arm had tightened. In a moment she would scream with pain. But that was not all. The Queen was threatening her with a beating if she did not say a welcome to her governess. Mary had a vision of herself being ignobly beaten in front of the other children with one of Madame de Paroy's canes. It would be too humiliating.

She said sullenly: 'Welcome, Madame de Paroy.'

The grip on her arm relaxed.

Catherine was smiling.

'Good,' she murmured. 'Very good. I think, Madame de Paroy, that in time we shall teach the Queen of Scotland that she is not yet the ruler of France.'

7

The Royal Wedding

That was the beginning of change. The old easy-going pleasurable ways were over. The weeks which followed were almost intolerable as Madame de Paroy was determined to please her mistress, and she could best do that by terrorizing the other children while she subdued Mary's proud spirit.

Many beatings were administered – and Mary received more than her share. It was an extra humiliation that these should be witnessed by the others, and during those first weeks Mary was very unhappy.

But when the King returned to Saint-Germain and saw how matters were he did his best to make them better.

He did not dismiss Madame de Paroy, because that would be flouting the Queen's authority and a breach of etiquette – something which must never happen at the French Court; but he did declare himself to be dissatisfied with the lessons the children were receiving, and he appointed his sister Marguerite to superintend these. This meant that they saw less of Madame de Paroy although she still remained in the nurseries.

When Mary met the Princess Marguerite she took one look at her and loved her, for the Princess was gentle, kind, and so like the King that almost immediately she was given that place in Mary's heart which had been Lady Fleming's.

Then the months began to pass more peaceably and even Madame de Paroy seemed less significant.

Mary was becoming more and more French. She spoke the language fluently now; her manners were French, and so were her clothes; and as she was growing up all the early promises of beauty were fulfilled.

It was generally accepted that she was the loveliest girl at the French Court.

During the next years she saw less of Queen Catherine, for the Queen bore many children and one by one these joined the nurseries.

Claude and Louis had been babies when Mary had arrived in France, and poor little Louis died in infancy. But young Charles, Edouard Alexandre, and Marguerite had been born and duly made their appearance in the nurseries.

Claude was quiet like Elisabeth but the three younger children had widely differing characteristics. First there was young Charles who, from the moment he had been aware of her, had been Mary's devoted slave. He was an odd boy, given to sudden rages which left him sullen. Then there was Edouard Alexandre, who was always called Henry by his mother; he resembled her more than any of the other children did, and it was said in the Court that he was a real Italian. He was very handsome with his olive skin, black hair and flashing eyes; he loved bright colours and was aware of clothes at a very early age. 'More like a girl than a boy,' said the courtiers. Once he took one of his mother's earrings and put it in his ear; he was discovered before a mirror admiring himself; and although any of the other children would have been whipped by Catherine for such folly, she merely laughed at her favourite Henry and gave him the other earring so that he had a pair; and much to the astonishment of everyone he was rarely seen without them. Marguerite – known as Margot – was bright, pert and very pretty, and always in some mischief; and lastly there was the baby, Hercule.

With the birth of each child there had been great celebrations, for the King was always delighted when there was a new baby.

The nurseries were extended considerably as these children grew up, because the King thought it would be a good idea if members of the leading families of France sent their children to be brought up with the royal family. This was done and very soon there were thirty young people all sharing lessons, and having a household of their own. They had their own doctors, apothecaries and barbers; and their cooks were kept busy feeding them and the huge staff of servants. They ate a great deal, in accordance with the fashion of the day, and two hundred and seventy-six loaves were baked and eaten each day; four calves, eight sheep and twenty capons were eaten daily; and of course much more was consumed besides.

The children's apartments had become a separate establishment, and as she grew older Mary still remained the leading figure in that little world. Moreover she learned to avoid trouble with Madame de Paroy and eventually accepted the irritation of having her in the suite.

There were always her beloved Marys with whom to share

her triumphs and troubles, so she had plenty of confidantes. The friendship between herself and the Dauphin grew stronger, which was particularly pleasant, Mary often told herself, because it was frequently the fate of royal people to have to leave their homes and go far away to a new country when they married.

Her mother had paid the promised visit to France and it had been a great joy to see her again.

The visit passed all too quickly, and Mary of Guise had to return to the turbulent land of Scotland, but before she left she told her daughter how happy she was to know that she now regarded France as her home.

Often Mary was in the company of Uncle Francis and Uncle Charles. The former, since the death of his father, had become the Duke of Guise. They continued to be pleased with her and constantly urged her not to allow her influence over the Dauphin to diminish.

That seemed unlikely, for young Francis was never happy unless he was in her company. When they went out hunting with the Court he was always at her side; when he felt tired – which he often did – at a ball or banquet, Mary would notice this and make some excuse for them to slip away. In all the years she never forgot that she had come to France to look after him, and she was as determined to do this as she ever had been.

They were now about fifteen years old and were scarcely seen apart.

One day when they were out riding with the Court the Dauphin felt one of his dizzy spells coming on and he dropped behind the others, to be joined immediately by Mary. She brought her horse close to his and, seeing that he was indeed ill, she leaped out of the saddle and caught him just as he would have fallen.

He recovered in a few seconds.

'It was only the usual dizziness,' he said.

'Nevertheless you must not ride any more today,' Mary told him. 'We are going back to the Palace.'

'But you must go on. I can go back alone.'

She laughed at him. 'As if I should allow that! Of course I am coming back. And there is only one way in which my day could be spoilt. That is if you were not with us.'

Francis's pale cheeks flushed with pleasure and he cried: 'Oh Mary, I should not want to live without you.'

'Then that is well,' she told him gaily, 'because as we are to be married it is good that you like my company.'

But when they reached the Palace Mary insisted on calling a physician to the Dauphin, who was kept in his apartments for the rest of the day. Mary stayed with him, reading to him, talking to him; and when the hunting party returned with the King at its head, it became known throughout the Court that the Dauphin had been indisposed during the hunt and that Mary had brought him back to the Palace.

The King was worried and spent a long time closetted with the physician who had examined his son.

A rumour went round the Palace then that young Francis was very delicate, and it might very well be that his young brother Charles would be the next to ascend the throne.

When Mary's Uncle Charles, the Cardinal of Lorraine, heard of the Dauphin's indisposition, he paid a hurried visit to his brother Francis, the Duke of Guise.

'A pretty state of affairs,' he said, 'if the Dauphin should die before the marriage. Mary would never then have a chance of being Dauphine – nor Queen of France.'

'We might arrange a marriage between her and Prince Charles – if young Francis should die.'

'Charles is nearly ten years younger than she is!'

The Duke of Guise lifted his shoulders. 'When he is a little older that would seem a small matter. The boy adores her and would be willing.'

'It's true,' the Cardinal replied, 'and should Francis die and Charles become Dauphin that will be the time to bring this about. In the meantime I should like to hurry on the wedding. They are scarcely children now.'

'Nearly sixteen,' mused the Duke. 'Yes, I think the time has come.'

'It would be well if you approached the King and suggested that there should be no more delay.'

'I will do this,' answered the Duke; and he left his brother and went straight to the King's apartments where he begged for an audience.

The King sent word that he would receive the Duke at once, which was gratifying to Francis, but when he arrived in the King's presence and saw that Queen Catherine was with the King he was not so pleased.

'Pray state your business, cousin,' said the King.

The Duke hesitated but, like most people at Court he believed that Queen Catherine was of little importance, so he began: 'Your Majesties, my business concerns my niece, and the Dauphin. They are such close friends, and no longer children. It is my belief – and I am sure Your Majesties will agree with me – that they are ripe for marriage. A marriage now would please not only them but the people of France. Mary Stuart would be a beautiful Dauphine.'

'That is true enough,' put in the Queen. 'We constantly hear praises sung of her beauty and charm. She will certainly be a beautiful Dauphine – when she is ready for marriage.'

'She is ready now,' said the Duke whose attention was for the King, not the Queen.

'They are children still,' insisted the Queen. 'We should not forget that. You, Your Majesty, and you, Monsieur de Guise, must tell me if I am wrong, but it seems to me that this charming friendship between these two might be spoilt by a different relationship. We all wish them every happiness in the world, but to marry two children while they are as yet children could be disastrous. I remember myself—'

She was looking at the King and recalling to him their own first meeting. She, a plain girl from Italy, he a shy boy

who hated the thought of marrying anyone, most all the
bride who had been chosen for him. He had become reconciled to marriage now, which was natural; but he remembered the painful period which had elapsed before this had
come about.

He said: 'They should wait a year.'

The Queen visibly relaxed and a smile touched her heavy
features. The Duke was so angry with her that he could have
slapped that smile off her face.

Being hot tempered he could not control his rage and said:
'These two are ready for marriage. In my opinion ...'

'Pray spare us your opinion,' the King interrupted coldly.
'It is of small moment, since it is not that of myself and the
Queen.'

He waved his hand to dismiss the Duke who could only
bow and retire. As he did so, however, he was aware of the
sly triumph on the face of the Queen.

The Duke had returned to his brother in a state of great
fury. 'It was all due to the Queen,' he cried. 'She is against
the marriage. I would not have believed she had so much
influence with the King. So we must wait a year – and, with
Francis's health as it is, who knows what will happen in a
year!'

'We will not despair,' soothed the Cardinal. 'Nor shall we
allow ourselves to be put out by Madame Catherine. I understand her game. She longs for power. Make no mistake,
brother. Behind that smug face of hers lies the longing to
rule. She would not be sorry if Francis died tomorrow because he is completely under Mary's influence, and absolutely devoted to her. Therefore if he ever became King, we
should rule – for we should advise Mary, who in her turn
would advise him.'

'The King has many years left to him.'

'Indeed yes. But the Dauphin of France is not without
power. We have two tasks before us, brother: to keep Francis
alive and to marry him to Mary. I have a little plan which

may succeed. I shall go to see the King now, and I shall not lay my plan before him if the Queen is with him. This is for his ears alone.'

'What is this plan?'

'We shall shortly be needing the help of Scotland against the English. They would be more ready to give it if the Queen of Scotland were also Dauphine of France. That is one point. Another is that, in exchange for a marriage contract, Mary could sign an agreement that, should she die without heirs, Scotland would pass to the French crown.'

'She has no power to do this.'

'She is the Queen of Scotland and her signature would make such an agreement valid.'

'She would never sign it.'

'You leave that to me,' replied the Cardinal.

The Duke looked at his brother in silence. He was only a bluff soldier, he realized; the Cardinal was a sly diplomatist. He was ready to use the crown of Scotland in his game of power politics – moreover he was ready to use his niece Mary. And all this that the Guises might one day rule France through their niece! What they wanted was to be the power behind the throne.

The Cardinal came to Mary's apartment and sent away her Marys who were with her, because that which he had to say was for her alone.

He had brought her presents – some silk to be made into a gown, some scent which was like that with which he perfumed his own linen.

'How kind you are to me, Uncle Charles!' she cried excitedly.

'Who would not be kind to a niece who is the most beautiful girl at Court?'

'Like most people you flatter me, Uncle.'

'No one could flatter you, Mary, because you are in truth as charming as we say you are. Francis is delighted that he is soon to be your husband, is he not?'

'Yes. He says that when we are married we shall be closer still.'

'If a son were born to you, that boy would one day be King of France,' said the Cardinal. 'Have you thought of that?'

'I had not. But of course it is true.'

'It would be wonderful. He would have Guise blood in him. My kinsman would be King of France!'

The Cardinal saw himself ruling through the son of Mary and Francis. That was the culmination of his dream. But they were not married yet and, although Mary was healthy, Francis was not. So much depended on chance.

Still, the first step was about to be taken. He had persuaded the King to agree to the marriage – for a consideration. And it was for this reason that he was with Mary now.

'You are excited about your wedding, eh?' he asked. 'You are thinking about your gown and the pageants afterwards?'

'Oh yes, I have been talking about them with all the children. They are very excited about the parts they are going to play in it.'

'Excellent. But there are one or two tiresome formalities which have to be gone through as well as all the interesting things, you know.'

'I suppose so.'

'I wish you to put your signature to a document which I am going to take you to sign in a few moments.'

'What document is this?'

'Oh – just a tiresome paper.'

'I shall have to read it, shall I not? One should always know what one is signing, I believe.'

'There is no need for you to read this. I have read it for you. It is in legal language which I fear you would not readily understand. As you know, the King of France has done a great deal for you.'

'I do know it, and I shall never cease to love him for it.'

'He has also given a great deal of money for the defence of

Scotland. This paper will say that when you have opportunity of repaying him you will do so.'

'Gladly would I sign that,' declared Mary.

'I knew you would. You are so proud. You would always wish to pay your debts. Let us go now to the chamber where the King will be waiting for us, and you shall sign this document.'

The Cardinal took her then into that chamber where the King and certain witnesses were waiting.

And blithely, not knowing to what she was putting her name, in that sunny chamber at Fontainebleau Mary signed away that which she had no right to give.

Mary stood before the mirror while her Marys and several of her attendants bustled about her, every now and then pausing to look at the radiant reflection rapturously.

Mary was being dressed for her wedding in her apartments in the house of the Archbishop of Paris where she, with the royal family, had spent the night.

Flem and Livy were chattering away in French – a language which after so many years in France they looked on as their own. Beaton was saying that there was only one person in France who was not delighted because of the wedding, and that was the Queen of France.

'And,' she whispered to Seton, 'what do we care about her? She is of no importance.'

Seton looked solemn for a moment and then replied: 'We said that long ago. And look how she had Flem's mother sent back and the hateful Madame de Paroy put in her place!'

They were silent for some seconds remembering, and Seton thought how much happier she would have been if she could have said everyone, including the Queen Catherine, was delighted by the wedding.

But this was no day to brood on possible trouble. There was Mary, in her bridal gown of white damask which was ablaze with jewels, looking lovelier than she ever had looked before. Her mantle was made of velvet in a blue-grey shade and studded with pearls; on her lovely hair was a crown of pearls and diamonds, rubies and sapphires; and in the centre of this crown hung a large carbuncle which, as Flem whispered to Livy in an awed voice, was alone worth five hundred thousand crowns.

'There never could have been a more lovely bride!' sighed Livy.

But as Mary looked at her reflection she was not thinking of herself but of her bridegroom. Francis would certainly be nervous; he had never really liked being the centre of a great ceremony, and all eyes would assuredly be on him today. She would have to reassure him, look after him, make him see that the trappings of ceremony were not important as long as they loved each other.

With all the talk and bustle going on in the apartment no one noticed the door open and a small figure come in, until he was standing by Mary's side.

'Charles!' cried Mary. 'What are you doing here?'

The young Prince looked sullen. 'I wanted to see you, that's all,' he said.

'You will see enough of me today, I'll warrant,' laughed Mary.

'I can never see enough of you,' said the boy angrily.

'You must not be angry on your brother's wedding day,' Mary told him.

'But it is because it is his wedding day that I am angry,' Charles retorted.

'Oh, you will have a wedding day when you are old enough.'

Charles stamped his foot and his face grew purple. Mary, who knew that he could fly into sudden rages, fervently hoped he was not going to do so now.

'It is not because it is his wedding day that I am angry. It is because you will be his bride. If I had been my father's eldest son I, not Francis, would have married you. How much better that would have been! I am strong and well. I do not grow tired after a few minutes. How I hate Francis for being my elder brother!'

'That is very wrong, Charles.'

'I don't care!' cried Charles.

Beaton came over. 'Is anything amiss?' she asked.

'Everything is wrong,' screamed Charles, 'because my brother Francis is my father's eldest son and I am not.'

The four Marys were alarmed. It would be unfortunate if Charles flew into one of his mad rages and lay on the floor kicking everyone who tried to approach him, as he had been known to do. And on Mary's wedding day!

Mary read their thoughts, and indeed they were also hers. She went close to Charles and laid her hand pleadingly on his arm. 'Charles, she said gently, 'please be calm. It is no use railing against what is, is it? Francis is your father's eldest son and therefore heir to the crown. Getting angry won't alter that.'

Charles took her hand and kissed it. 'When he dies,' he said, 'will you marry me?'

Mary smiled, seeing the way to placate him. 'Of course,' she said; and the smile which took the place of his scowl would have been disconcerting if she had more time to think about it.

'It's a promise,' he said; and she nodded.

'Now please, Charles, go back to your apartment. I am not ready, and I must be. So must you.'

'Dear Mary,' said the boy, 'I always want to please you.'

When he had gone she raised her eyebrows and smiled at the Marys. 'Cheer up,' she commanded. 'You look as though you're going to a funeral rather than a wedding. What's the matter, Flem? You're trembling. And you, Seton! You look as though you've seen a ghost.'

'It seemed like an evil omen ... promising to marry Charles on your wedding day to Francis,' Flem pointed out.

'Nonsense!' cried Mary. 'Charles is only a boy. He's jealous because his brother is having a wedding, that's all. Now, Seton, what are *you* thinking?'

'Only that I hope and pray that *is* all,' said Seton.

It was the King himself who held Mary's right hand as he conducted her along the gallery which had been erected between the Archbishop's Palace and the Cathedral of Notre Dame. Her left hand was held by her kinsman, the Duke of Lorraine.

When they reached the door of the Cathedral they halted, and were there joined by the Dauphin escorted by the King of Navarre who had come to Paris for the wedding.

Mary noticed that Francis's two brothers, Charles and Edouard Alexandre, were with him. She could not prevent her eyes going anxiously to Charles who was staring at her fixedly; and a fear came to her that Charles might be crazy enough to make a scene there at the door of the Cathedral under the eyes of all the people.

He certainly looked very sullen, but when she smiled at him his expression changed at once; and into his face there came a secretive look as though he and Mary shared something which was for no one but themselves.

Now it was time for the marriage to take place, and the King took from his finger a ring which scintillated in the sunlight; this he handed to the Cardinal de Bourbon, who took it and performed the sacred rites in the open so that all the people who had gathered there to see the ceremony should not be disappointed.

As Francis and Mary joined hands a shout went up from the people:

'*Vive le Dauphin! Vive la Dauphine!*'

The procession made its way back to the Bishop's Palace for the wedding banquet; now the solemnity was over and the jollifications began.

Francis was too nervous to eat, and Mary had to persuade him that there was nothing to fear.

When the feasting was over, the King asked Mary to dance with him; and so they opened the ball.

Mary's cheeks were flushed, her eyes bright, as she danced with the King, and he watched her with loving admiration.

'Francis is very lucky,' he said, 'to have such a bride.'

'And I to have such a husband,' she answered.

'Ah yes – he will one day bring you the crown of France.'

Mary could never hide her emotions, and she could not then; her face showed the pain she felt. 'Father,' she said, 'do not speak of our being King and Queen. Have you forgotten what must happen before we can wear the crown?'

The King smiled at her tenderly. 'It cannot be yours until I am dead.'

'Please – please do not speak of such a thing!' Indignation had crept into her voice. 'Do you think that I would wish to lose my Father that I might gain a crown?'

He took her hand and kissed it, and she saw too that he was overcome with emotion. 'It is rarely,' he said, 'that a King is loved for himself.'

Looking up then, Mary saw Francis who, because she was dancing with the King, must dance with the Queen; he looked very unhappy dancing with Catherine.

The King was saying gently: 'You will look after my son Francis, Mary. He will need constant care, and I know I can trust you. Promise me now that you will always love him and, if I should not be here, protect him – should the need arise.'

'I promise, Father.'

It was the second promise, apart from her marriage vows, which she had made that day – the first lightly to young Charles, but this to the King was made with the utmost solemnity.

A wedding must be a joyous occasion; and when the ball at the Bishop's Palace was over, the party formed a magnificent procession and crossed the Seine to the Palais de Justice where another feast was prepared for them, with an entertainment to follow.

In this all the royal children took part, riding on hobby horses caparisoned with gold and silver and pulled across the floor by lackeys. When the hobby horses reached the spot where Francis and Mary were sitting they stopped, and the Princes and Princesses sang songs of praise to the couple; and all the time Mary was aware of Charles's face distorted by envy.

Later in the evening galleons were brought into the ball-room to glide over the floor while an artificial breeze ruffled their silver gauze sails. The ships were led by lackeys and the first and most magnificent of them paused before Mary. Then she saw that the King, who had a short while before, disappeared from the ballroom, was seated in this galleon and was asking her to join him. This she did joyfully, and then she saw that in the next galleon Francis was forced to sit with his mother. In the other galleons members of the royal family were seated, and over the ballroom floor they glided.

But all the time Mary was conscious of her bridegroom who must be the companion of the sly Queen, while she herself enjoyed the company of the charming King.

It was symbolic in a way. In spite of all the gaiety and brilliance there were undercurrents of evil. It was there in the sullen eyes of Charles, the sly ones of Catherine who had tried to prevent the marriage and was now behaving as though she was pleased about it; and also in the alert eyes of Mary's uncles, who saw this wedding as a step nearer to that day when they would be the real rulers of France.

8

The Tragic Joust

Now Mary, as Dauphine, had her own household and greater honour and prestige than she had ever had before.

'The first thing I shall do,' she gleefully told Francis, 'is to dismiss Madame de Paroy. Don't you think that is a good idea?'

Francis nodded. He thought all Mary's ideas good ones.

He was very happy, being married to Mary. It meant they were always together in their own small Court which was made up of those whom they chose. The four Marys were of course constantly in attendance on the Dauphine, and they all took advantage of the greater freedom they now enjoyed.

Mary exuberantly decided how the days should be spent. When the Dauphin was not too tired they joined the hunt; remembering her promise to his father, Mary always made his health her first consideration. There were further balls to celebrate the marriage, and life was one long round of gaiety. Nothing could have been more acceptable to Mary. Alas, poor Francis longed for a quieter life. Soon after the wedding they went to the lovely old château at Villers-Cotterets for their honeymoon and, because they were almost alone there, Francis was happier than he had ever been before. This was the life which he loved, partly because he had Mary all to himself, partly because it did not tire him. It was very pleasant to walk in the beautiful countryside, or ride through the woods; or perhaps sit watching the fountains play while Mary read to him. Francis would have liked to go on in that way for ever. But, of course, the Dauphin and Dauphine had to return to Court.

There, people – with few exceptions – were prepared to pet and pamper Mary. Even those who were envious of her charm and beauty remembered that one day she might be Queen of France, and therefore flattered her. Had she not been fundamentally the most generous person imaginable, this might have spoiled her; but much as she loved flattery and beautiful clothes and jewels, she would never willingly be unkind to anyone – unless they attacked her first – and she was constantly putting herself into other people's places, which meant that she invariably saw their point of view.

One day Uncle Francis and Uncle Charles came to her apartments in a state of great excitement.

'News from England!' announced Uncle Francis, his eyes gleaming and the scar on his cheek, inflicted in battle, which had earned him the name of *Le Balafré*, standing out more than usual.

'Queen Mary of England is dead,' explained Uncle Charles, 'and the crown has been taken by Elizabeth, who has no right to it.'

'But she is the daughter of King Henry VIII and sister to Queen Mary. She was next in the line of succession.'

'Elizabeth has no right to the throne,' cried Uncle Francis in a voice of thunder. 'The union between her mother, Anne Boleyn, and Henry VIII was no true marriage. Therefore you are next in line of succession. It is you, Mary, who should be Queen of England. Are you not a great-grand-daughter of King Henry VII?'

'But you say Elizabeth has already taken the throne,' said Mary.

'I am going straight to the King,' Uncle Francis said, 'and ask him to give me men and arms. Then I shall go to England and win for you what this Elizabeth has tried to take from you.'

'But, Uncle, as I am Queen of Scotland and Dauphine of France, what do I want with the crown of England?'

Both her uncles were aghast. Uncle Francis looked disgusted, Uncle Charles disappointed.

'My dear Mary,' the latter said, 'all these balls and banquets have put you in a frivolous mood. I am surprised. Naturally, the more your possessions, the greater your power. No one in the world can be too powerful.'

Mary sighed; now, like Francis, she was longing for the peace of Villers-Cotterets.

She was secretly pleased when the King refused to send the Duke of Guise to England with men and arms to fight for the crown of England. But the King, like her uncles, believed that the crown of England should be hers; so, from that time, 'Queen of England' was added to her titles and she was required to display the armorial bearings of England.

Thus at all functions she was announced as 'Dauphine of France, Queen of England and Queen of Scotland and the Isles.'

Mary shrugged her shoulders, believing that it mattered little what they called her.

One day Mary noticed the Princess Elisabeth, who had always been her good friend since the days of their first meeting, looking very sad.

Elisabeth was a pale, pretty girl of quiet manners; both she and Claude were very different from their youngest sister, the naughty little Margot.

Mary asked her what ailed her, and Elisabeth said: 'Come for a walk with me in the gardens, and I will tell you.'

So together they strolled through the lovely gardens of Fontainebleau, and Elisabeth told Mary of her trouble.

'You know we have been at war with Spain and that my father is now anxious to make peace. Well, the treaty is being made and one of the clauses is that I am to go to Spain as bride to the King.'

'Oh, Elisabeth! So you will go away from us all.'

Elisabeth turned away and studied the fountains through a haze of tears.

'Away from you all – away from my home – to a strange land.'

Mary was filled with compassion.

'Have you spoken to Father about it?' she asked.

'Yes. He it was who told me. He said he did not want it to come from anyone else. Philip of Spain is a widower and he has asked for my hand. I am to marry him. It has all been settled.'

'But Philip of Spain—' murmured Mary.

'Yes. It is not only that I have to leave home, but I must marry this man who has had two wives already.'

'I know. The Queen of England was one of them.'

Elisabeth nodded. 'And when she died he needed another wife. I am to fill that role.'

It was particularly sad, because Mary had heard – and she was sure Elisabeth had too – that Philip of Spain was a melancholy man who rarely smiled. Poor, poor Elisabeth!

And what could Mary do to comfort her? The King of France was kind but it was no use appealing to him. It was the fate of all Princes and Princesses to marry whoever was chosen for them and do whatever was necessary for the welfare of their country.

Elisabeth turned to Mary, and Mary saw that she was crying quietly.

Now there were preparations for another wedding. How different this was from the Dauphin's marriage. Poor Elisabeth grew more and more like a wraith each day. She was so pale and thin that Mary feared she would waste away.

Elisabeth was now sixteen years old and that, she had been told by her mother, was old enough to marry. Mary never saw Elisabeth cry again after that incident in the gardens of Fontainebleau; the bride-to-be seemed as though she were steeling herself for an ordeal.

There was to be yet another marriage at the Court, and this too was distressing. The Princess Marguerite, the King's sister who had been such a kind and helpful governess and who had done much to rescue the royal children from the intolerable rule of Madame de Paroy, was to marry the Duke of Savoy; and this marriage had been arranged as part of the same treaty which allied Elisabeth with King Philip of Spain.

'So,' mourned Mary to the Dauphin, 'we shall lose not only Elisabeth but Aunt Marguerite as well.'

As the summer approached, so the time came nearer when Elisabeth must leave for Spain, and at length the Duke of Alva came to stand as proxy for Philip, because the great King of Spain would not come to fetch his bride; she must go to him. Elisabeth was pleased about this because it put off the evil hour of meeting a little longer.

The Duke of Savoy, however, who was to be Princess Marguerite's husband, did come to France, and great pageants were arranged in honour of him and his suite, together with the envoys from Spain.

One hot June day a tournament had been arranged to

take place in Paris. The arena had been set up in Les Tournelles and as soon as it was light crowds began to gather in
the Rue St Antoine.

The carriage which would take Mary and Francis to the
arena was waiting for them when they left their apartments,
and on it, the armorial bearings of England were vivid in the
sunlight; people cheered them as slowly they drove through
the crowds which had assembled for the tournament.

'*Vive la Dauphin!*' they cried. '*Vive la Dauphine!*'

Mary smiled in acknowledgement. Francis scarcely looked
at them; he was not really indifferent, Mary wanted to
exlain, only shy.

'Make place! Make place for the Queen of England,'
shouted the heralds; and Mary thought fleetingly of her
cousin of England who, she had heard, was red-headed and
arrogant. It is a mercy, thought Mary, that she cannot hear
them.

They took their places in the arena. Queen Catherine was
already in the royal gallery. She gave them her sly smile and
Mary was sure that she noticed how pale Francis was looking;
and was that satisfaction she saw in the flat face? Surely not.
The Queen was after all Francis' mother. If he were ill she
must be anxious on his account. But it was impossible to
guess what went on behind those heavy features.

All the royal children arrived and Charles, sullen as ever,
slipped into the seat next to Mary.

Now the jousting had begun and all the most noble of the
men at the Court entertained the company with their
brilliant play. The foreign guests joined in the sport and at
last it was time for the King to ride into the arena.

This was the greatest excitement of the day, for all those
people, who had been waiting for hours, wanted most of all
to see their King win a victory over his opponent.

He was a father to be proud of, thought Mary, as she
watched him ride, his armour glittering like silver in the
sunshine, and his spurs twinkling with jewels.

He was riding a magnificent white horse which had been a

gift to him from Marguerite's fiancé, the Duke of Savoy; and he could not have had a more fitting mount. He looked and rode like a King.

The tilting began; the King was more skilled than his opponent. The crowds roared their delight when, with an accomplished gesture, the King crashed his lance against the other's so successfully that rider and horse were completely at his mercy.

Victory for the King! He had acquitted himself with honour, and the people were well pleased.

But, instead of returning to his place in the royal gallery, the King said he would like to joust once more and, looking about him, he singled out one of the champions of the joust, a young man named Montgomery who was a captain of the Scottish guard, and challenged him to joust.

The King's horse was sweating with the exertion of the previous encounter; as for the King himself, he was less fresh naturally than he had been an hour before. Montgomery noticed this and, because he believed he would defeat the King, he would have preferred not to be his opponent.

He hesitated, and the King, realizing the reason, insisted that he could beat him; so there was nothing the captain could do but obey and accept the King's challenge.

Then the trumpets sounded and the King was galloping down the lists, his lance extended.

Mary was never quite sure how it happened. She saw the two men meet, their lances clash, and then the King was falling from his horse.

Lying on a litter the King was carried into the Palace of the Tournelles, his face covered with a cloth. When his helmet had been removed it was discovered that the captain's lance had shivered into many pieces and one of these had entered the King's right eye.

There was sorrow throughout the Court. For ten days the King had lain on his bed in great pain and unable to speak, for no one knew how to remove the splinter from his eye.

Mary went to the nursery where all the children were waiting, and while they sat together a messenger came to tell them that they must all go to the King's bedside.

Mary tried not to believe that they were going to say good-bye to the dearest of fathers.

There lay the King, so still that they feared he was already dead. He did not speak to them, he did not even know that they were there; his breathing came heavily and the last rites were administered.

In the room next to the bedchamber all the important men of France were gathering, and among them Mary saw her uncles who nodded acknowledgement when they caught her eye. Because she knew them so well, she realized that they were doing their best to suppress the excitement they were feeling.

They want him dead! she thought; and in that moment she came near to hating them. This was the one she loved – this dear father who was lying on his death bed – not the uncles who had schemed to use her to increase their power.

'Oh Father, dearest Father,' she murmured, 'you must not die. Francis cannot be King. He is too young and weak. Besides, we love you so much.'

She felt the warm tears on her cheeks, and she saw the figure on the bed through a mist of tears.

Someone murmured: 'The King is dead. Long live the King!'

Francis, standing beside Mary, began to tremble because he realized that not only had he lost the father whom he had loved but that father's burdens had been laid upon his shoulders, shoulders which were not strong enough to bear them.

They were all filing out of the chamber of death. Francis went first and Queen Catherine and Mary were side by side. Mary stood aside, as she had on so many other occasions, for

Catherine to pass her. But Catherine paused, then stretching out a hand she pushed Mary ahead of her.

Mary understood. Now she must take precedence over Queen Catherine, because Catherine was merely the Queen Mother while Mary was now the Queen of France.

9

Death at the Balliage

King Francis II was a frightened king. Every morning when he awoke he would tremble to think of what new terrors the day held for him. If it were not for Mary he believed he would die. But Mary was always at his side, always ready to protect him, always ready to comfort him.

He mourned his father's death with greater sorrow than anyone else at Court. Others had loved Henry II but to Francis he had been more than loving father, kind companion, friendly adviser. He had carried all the burdens of kingship which on his death must fall on Francis.

No one left him alone for long. His mother was more interested in him than she had ever been before. The Duke of Guise and the Cardinal of Lorraine came to him and told him that he need have no fear; *they* would be beside him, *they* would advise him and comfort him. The Cardinal of Lorraine assured him that he would be as a father to him. And the two people who, more than any others in France terrified Francis, were his mother and the Cardinal of Lorraine.

'I feel,' he told Mary, 'like a bone over which fierce dogs are fighting. There is my mother on one side and your uncles on the other.'

'My uncles only want to help you,' she assured him.

'They want to rule this country,' Francis answered. 'So does my mother. It is power they all want. They do not love us, Mary. They only love power.'

Mary knew there was some truth in this, but she found it difficult to believe ill of her uncles who, all her life, had been held up to her as symbols of valour and wisdom. If it were a case of quarrels between her uncles and Queen Catherine, every time she would be on the side of her uncles because she hated Catherine as much as she ever had; and because Francis always took Mary's advice and endeavoured to please her in every possible way, in a very short time it became obvious that the Queen Mother had no power over her son, because Mary was determined that she should not.

The English ambassador wrote to the Queen of England: 'The House of Guise rules France—'

This was true. It was a state of affairs which was unacceptable to Queen Catherine and she was determined to change it.

'One cannot mourn for ever. Life must go on.' So said Queen Catherine, and those words filled her daughter Elisabeth with foreboding of evil, because she knew that her mother meant that, even though her father was dead, that sad event would make no difference to her future, and the preparations for her departure for Spain must go on.

Poor Elisabeth! Mary tried to comfort her. But what could she do? What comfort was there for the young Princess?

Life was no longer carefree for Mary since King Henry had died. She was finding it more and more difficult to obey her uncles, and her young husband had confessed to her that he hated the Cardinal of Lorraine. As for the Cardinal, he had called Francis a coward on more than one occasion.

Moreover the people did not love the new King as they had loved his father. When he rode among them he appeared sullen, and they rarely cried '*Vive le roi!*' as they had done in the old days. There were rumours in circulation that the young King was suffering from a wasting disease and that he was only kept alive by drinking the blood of freshly killed babies.

When Francis passed through the towns and villages, mothers hid their children. That was what hurt Francis more than anything. He was gentle by nature; he hated killing a fly; and that his people should think for one moment that he would harm their children wounded him deeply.

So the King of France was one of the saddest people in the land.

Mary knew this but she never confided in anyone but her own four Marys.

One one of these occasions Seton said: 'Have you noticed what care the Queen Mother is taking of Charles? Sometimes I think—'

It was so rarely that Seton spoke impulsively that Mary insisted that she continue with what she was about to say. 'Well,' said Seton reluctantly, 'I thought she seemed as though she was brooding – waiting for the time when Charles will be King, and that she would be rather pleased if Charles could be King.'

'But he could only be King if—' cried Livy.

'Yes,' Mary interrupted, 'only if Francis *died*.'

It was a dangerous subject and the cautious Seton was looking furtively over her shoulder as though she feared they might be overheard. Yes, indeed it was dangerous. But it must be remembered that Francis, through Mary, had become the tool of the Guises. If Charles were King he would be controlled by his mother. The power behind the throne then would be, not the Guises, but Queen Catherine.

Mary shivered. Everyone was aware that the Italians knew more about secret poisons than any other people; and there were rumours throughout the Court that the Queen Mother was an expert in this 'art'.

Mary had to protect Francis from his fears and his own nervousness. Must she protect him from his mother also?

The Court had reached the château of Chenonceaux, one of the loveliest in the whole of France, which was built on a bridge and gave the impression of floating on water.

Mary's pleasure was spoilt, however, because the reason for their stay here was such a sad one. The royal party was conducting Elisabeth to the borders of France and Spain, and at the frontier they would say goodbye to her – perhaps for ever. It was small wonder, therefore that they were all melancholy.

Moreover, Francis's health was not improving. He was now suffering from painful abscesses which kept forming in his ears, and as soon as one appeared to improve there would be another starting up. Mary had insisted that Dr Ambrose Paré, who was reckoned one of the cleverest doctors in France, should always be with them. The Queen Mother had laughed at what she called coddling, but Mary angrily reminded her that she was Queen of France and would decide what was best for the King.

Catherine had bowed her head in resignation, accepting the rebuke in her mild manner; and Paré travelled with them.

When they reached their apartments Francis was absolutely weary and his ear was so painful that Mary called Dr Paré to look at it.

The doctor was thoughtful and said that Francis should go straight to bed, when he would give him a soothing draught which would make him sleep.

This was done and Mary left him sleeping while she went to the adjoining room, there to be made ready for the supper which was being prepared for them.

The Marys came in to help her dress and, as she sat before the Venetian mirror and they combed her hair, the talk grew confidential.

'I heard,' said Flem, 'that the Queen Mother is very much afraid that you will have a son, Mary.'

Mary replied: 'She need have no fear.'

'If you did,' put in Beaton, 'it would mean Charles would never have the throne. That is what she fears.'

'It is strange,' mused Mary. 'She was always my enemy, from the time I came here. I suppose she always will be.'

Seton was standing by with Mary's blue velvet dress, waiting to slip it over her shoulders. It was disquieting to see how perturbed Seton now was.

'We should watch her very carefully,' said Seton suddenly. 'I am so glad Doctor Paré is with us.'

'You don't think Francis is worse?' cried Mary in alarm.

'Oh, he is merely tired with the journey,' said Flem and Beaton together.

It was time they joined the company assembling in the great hall. It was always thrilling to enter a room now where everyone must greet Mary as the Queen.

Now the crowd separated as she appeared, and all the men bowed and the women curtseyed as she passed by, smiling her gay and friendly smile, her Marys following her. As she took her place at the banqueting table Queen Catherine came and sat beside her.

'I am grieved that my son is too indisposed to come to the banquet.'

Mary looked into the expressionless eyes.

'It was nothing much,' she replied. 'He was merely fa-
tigued by the journey and is resting on Dr Paré's advice.'

The Queen Mother made the little puffing noise with her
lips. 'That doctor makes too much of too little. That has
always been my opinion.'

'I believe him to be the best doctor in France,' retorted
Mary coolly. 'I am determined that he shall be in constant
attendance on the King.'

'And you are the Queen of France, so your word is law,'
murmured the Queen Mother with one of her sudden
laughs.

Mary found that she was very hungry; she ate heartily and
chatted gaily with those about her as she did so; but when
the meal was over, the company rose to dance and as she was
led out by her partner to open the ball she felt suddenly
dizzy. Her knees buckled under her and it seemed as though
the room were spinning round.

She heard someone cry: 'The Queen has fainted . . .' before
she lost consciousness for a few seconds.

Then arms were about her, and she realized that she was
lying on the floor and that several people were bending over
her.

'What happened?' she asked.

'Your Majesty fainted for a second or so,' was the answer;
and Mary turned her head with revulsion because the arm
which held her was that of the Queen Mother.

Then she heard practical Beaton's voice. '*Aqua composita*
is what Her Majesty needs. I have some in my apartment. I
never travel without it.'

'Get it quickly,' commanded Queen Catherine.

'I feel better now,' murmured Mary. 'I can't think what
happened. It seemed so hot.'

'You should lie still,' advised Queen Catherine, and Mary
wanted to scream at her to take her arm away, and if she
must be supported, that someone else should do it. Then she
saw the calm eyes of Seton who was close by, and felt relieved.

'I should like to go to my apartment,' she said. 'I am a little tired, that is all.'

Seton was on her knees looking into her mistress's face. 'Beaton will be here with the *aqua* shortly. Your Majesty should take that and then you will feel strong enough to go to your room.'

Mary nodded and in a few minutes Beaton arrived with the *aqua* which was poured into a cup and given to her. When Mary had sipped it she felt revived and said that her four Marys should conduct her to her apartment, but she wanted the company to go on dancing.

'It is a command,' she said, reaching for Beaton's arm. Seton took Mary's other arm and with Flem and Livy she went to her own apartment, where they helped her to her bed.

'I am so tired,' she said; and they drew the scarlet damask curtains about the bed and left her to sleep.

Mary really was exhausted and at once she fell into a deep sleep. It seemed to her that she was almost immediately awakened by the sound of voices. She lay still, listening.

'But Madame, the Queen is sleeping.' That was Seton.

'It will be well to wake her that she may drink this. It will do her more good than anything else.'

The sound of that voice made Mary shudder because it was that of Queen Catherine.

'Madame,' replied Seton, 'it is the order of Dr Paré that she shall not be awakened.'

The order of Dr Paré! But Dr Paré had not seen her! What was Seton talking about?

'Nonsense. I tell you, my girl, that I know more of medicines than this doctor.'

'Madame, I dare not wake the Queen. Give me the potion and I will give it to her the moment the awakes.'

Mary closed her eyes quickly for she heard the swish of silk as the curtains were drawn aside.

'Wake up. I have come to make you well.'

She kept her eyes closed and was aware of a breath on her cheek and the sound of breathing very close to her. She felt as though some evil power was forcing her to open her eyes and being impelled to do so, saw Queen Catherine peering down at her and the frightened face of Seton behind her mother-in-law.

'I have brought you a potion which will make you perfectly well in a few minutes,' said Catherine.

'It is good of you,' answered Mary.

'Now drink it.' Catherine chuckled. 'I know you've never trusted me. Ha, it is because I am your mother-in-law, but that is foolish prejudice. We cannot have a sick Queen *and* a sick King. Come, my dear, this will put you right at once.'

She had leaned over the bed and had pulled Mary up so that she was in a sitting position. Seton's agonized eyes were flashing a warning. Mary knew what Seton meant: On no account drink the potion.

Mary said: 'I pray you put it by my bed. I feel so sick now that I could not drink it. Later I shall feel better.'

Relief shone from Seton's eyes. It was what she had been hoping for.

If Catherine was exasperated she did not show it; but then when had she ever shown her feelings? She seemed to come to a decision. She lifted a finger and said: 'You must take it as soon as you feel able to.'

Mary nodded, and lay back on her pillows while Catherine straightened the bedclothes. 'You should keep warm,' she said. 'And don't forget. Take the potion as soon as you are able.'

With that she went quietly away; and as soon as she had gone Seton picked up the goblet and stared into it.

'I want to throw it away quickly – before she returns,' said Seton, going to the window and throwing out the contents of the goblet.

'You're shivering, Seton,' said Mary when she came back to the bed.

'I was so afraid that you would drink it.'

'Do you believe she would poison me!'

'I think she is afraid that you may be going to have a child. If you did, that would spoil her hopes of seeing Charles on the throne.'

'Then you think she *would* poison me!'

'I do not know, but there are evil rumours about her. It is said that she had the King's elder brother poisoned so that her husband should be King. That was long ago and it may not be true – but it was said at the time of his death. I think we should be watchful.'

Then suddenly Seton's calmness deserted her. She threw herself on the bed and when Mary put her arms about her she felt the tremors that ran through her body.

They had said their last farewells to Elisabeth and she had gone on to Spain, vowing that she would remember them for the rest of her life, that she would write to them, and imploring them to write to her.

They travelled back to Saint-Germain and stayed there for a short while; and it was during one warm June day that sad news came for Mary.

Her mother, who had been ailing for some time, had died.

Mary mourned her sincerely, but it was ten years since the Dowager Queen had paid her visit to France, and Mary could scarcely remember what she looked like. She would sadly miss those tender and loving letters which were always full of good advice; and had she not been so worried about the health of her husband she would have been even more concerned. But, because she was so occupied with looking after him, she did not pause to wonder what effect the death of her mother might have on her future.

Those summer months were uneasy ones on account of Francis's failing health; the Court was always on the move and with the coming of winter was in the city of Orléans. Whenever the Court moved from place to place it took beds and furniture with it, for it was inconceivable that royal people could live without their possessions. Beds and tapestries were taken from château to château, so that moving around was a big undertaking. Moreover it was very necessary not to stay in any château for very long at a time, but to move away for what was called the 'sweetening' – which meant that the place had to be thoroughly cleaned in a manner which could not be done while the whole Court was in residence.

Francis's health had deteriorated sadly during the last months and the cold winds of the winter were particularly hard to endure.

An abscess in his ear had grown a great deal worse and he could not sleep because of the throbbing pain, nor could he rest by day.

Mary was very worried about him and kept Dr Paré in constant attendance.

The Court was staying in an old mansion in Orléans which was known by the name of the Balliage, and from here it was planned to move on to Chenonceaux.

The tapestries were being rolled up, the beds taken down, and meanwhile a bitterly cold north wind was blowing through the Balliage.

Francis came out accompanied by Mary. He looked very thin and pale and there was a bandage about his ear.

He was helped on to his horse, and Mary, who had followed him out, was about to mount when she saw that her young husband had slumped forward in the saddle. She called out in alarm and two of the attendants rushed forward just in time to prevent him slipping to the ground.

Queen Catherine came bustling up.

'The King has fainted,' Mary told her. 'He must be taken back. The beds must be replaced. The weather is too cold for him to travel. Dr Paré shall come to the King at once.'

She saw Queen Catherine looking at her son. Was there a hint of triumph in those eyes? Had Mary glimpsed something which the Queen Mother was trying to hide?

Seton came to tell Mary that Dr Paré was asking for a private audience with her.

Mary cried: 'Bring him to me without delay.'

But when he came, the Queen Mother was with him.

'I heard,' she said, 'that the doctor had something to tell you about the state of my son's health. I know you will understand that I am as anxious as you are.'

'Dr Paré,' said Mary earnestly, 'pray tell me what you have to. I cannot endure this suspense.'

'The King is gravely ill,' said the doctor. 'In fact, I do not think he can live many more days unless I operate.'

'An operation would save his life?' Catherine asked.

'That I cannot say, Madame. All I can tell you is that unless this operation is performed he will die.'

'Then the operation must be performed,' insisted Mary. 'It is better for him to take this chance of its being successful since, if he does not have it, he will die.'

Dr Paré turned to her. 'Then I must do the operation within the hour. After that it will certainly be too late.'

'Begin at once. Waste no more time.'

'One moment,' interrupted Catherine. 'My son has suffered much pain and I would not have him suffer more – unnecessarily.'

'But we must try to save his life,' cried Mary.

'There is no certainty that his life will be saved.'

'But don't you *see* – if there is no operation he will certainly die.'

'Dr Paré,' said Catherine, 'this is my son. His wife, the Queen, is very young. You must permit me a mother's privilege. Before I consent to your performing this operation there are certain questions I must ask you about it. I wish to speak to you alone.'

'I am the Queen,' interrupted Mary, 'and I believe this operation should be performed. I order that it be done.'

Catherine took a kerchief from the pocket of her gown and wiped the corner of her eye. 'It is useless to try to explain a mother's feelings. It was I who brought the King into the world. The Queen was the companion of his childhood, but he was my son before she ever came to France. Because I am his mother my consent is also necessary if this operation is to be performed, and I demand to speak alone with the doctor.'

Dr Paré looked from Mary to Catherine. Mary's face was swollen with weeping and she was frantic with anxiety; Catherine was calm, yet somehow she managed to convey an impression of grief.

'The operation must be performed within the hour,' he said to Mary. 'If you will allow me to speak – alone with the Queen Mother – I will convince her of the urgency.'

Mary nodded and went from the apartment to Francis's bedside.

Francis smiled wanly at her approach. 'Mary,' he whispered, 'I am glad you have come.'

'Francis,' she answered, 'we are going to save your life. You are going to be well again.'

Francis smiled, and she knew he did not believe her.

'It's true, Francis. You will get well. We are going to be so happy together.'

'Where are my mother and the Cardinal?' he asked, and she saw the fearful look in his eyes. 'They are not here, are they?'

'Only I am here at your bedside, Francis.'

'Please talk to me of the old days.'

So it was Mary who talked: she recalled her arrival in France all those years ago when she had first come to the nursery and found him and Elisabeth there; she reminded him of their walks in the gardens of Fontainebleau and their riding in the forest near Rambouillet, their wedding at Notre Dame and the honeymoon at Villers-Cotterets.

He smiled as she talked, and she believed that in remembering he forgot his pain a little.

She did not notice how the time was passing and it was an hour later when Dr Paré and Catherine came to the bedside.

She stood up and cried: 'You are going to operate now?'

Dr Paré was looking at the patient. He shook his head sadly and moved away from the bed. Mary ran after him

and, when he was out of earshot of the sick-bed, he whispered: 'You Majesty, it is too late – now nothing will avail.'

Catherine was behind him. 'Come quickly, Dr Paré. I believe I heard the death rattle.'

The doctor hurried to the bed and, as Mary looked at
Catherine, the Queen Mother's lips formed the words 'Too
late.'

Was there a touch of triumph in her face then? The
thought flashed into Mary's brain: You meant it to be too
late. You kept Dr Paré arguing so that it should be too late.
If that is so, in a way you are responsible for the death of
your son.

The King was dying. The last rites were being administered
and the wintry wind buffeted the walls of the Balliage. In
the chamber of death the chanting voices of priests mingled
with the mournful murmurings of men and women.

The Cardinal of Lorraine knelt by Francis's bed, while
Mary stood by sadly watching her husband. This was the
third tragedy in her life and it followed swiftly on the others.
Three people whom she had loved dearly were taken from
her: King Henry, her mother and now Francis. She felt suddenly desolate and alone.

The Queen Mother was at her side watching her closely.

'It is the end,' she whispered. 'The King is dead.'

The Cardinal was standing by the bed, looking down on
the dead boy. His face was twisted with an expression Mary
would not have understood a short while ago; but now she
knew that it had something to do with frustrated ambition.
There was a link between the unhappy looks of the Cardinal
and the faint triumph of the Queen Mother.

King Francis was dead, and that meant there was a new
King on the throne of France: King Charles, who was but a
boy and would be the tool of his mother, as Francis had been
the tool of the Guises.

Mary hated their ambitions; to her there could be nothing
but this great grief.

Francis is dead, dearest and gentlest of husbands; the boy, who had been her friend and adoring slave from the moment he had set eyes on her, had departed, leaving her lonely and sad.

Nothing, she thought, will ever be the same again; and tears blinded her as she walked towards the door. She was about to pass out when she felt herself suddenly thrust aside. Queen Catherine deftly stepped ahead of her, looking over her shoulder as she did so.

Mary understood. This was a reminder. With Francis dead she was no longer the first lady in the land. Catherine as Mother of the reigning King took precedence over the widow of the deceased King.

Mary knew that this was Catherine's final triumph. Had she not been so stricken with grief and unable to think of anything but the loss of Francis, she might have begun to be very apprehensive in that moment.

10

Home to Scotland and the Isles

Dressed entirely in white – white dress, white shoes, and flowing white veil – Mary remained shut away from the world for forty days and forty nights. This was the custom which all widowed Queens of France must follow; and during this period of seclusion she was allowed to see no one but her attendants and members of the royal family.

Mary was not sorry to observe this custom. She certainly

did not want to mingle with the people of the Court. She told herself during that period that she would continue to mourn Francis all her life.

Her Marys were with her and they did their best to comfort her; but she knew that they were wondering what would become of them all now.

Beaton had said that she believed they might have to go back to Scotland, because now that Mary's husband was dead there was no place for her in France – for although she still bore the title of Queen it was an empy title – and since her mother had died, there was work for her in Scotland. Perhaps now she would be called upon to rule the country in which she had been born.

Flem and Livy had been horrified at the suggestion. They had been so young when they had left Scotland that they could not remember much about it; but they did know that it was very different from the Court of France to which they had become accustomed.

They knew that there would not be the same gaiety, the same magnificence in the poor Court of Scotland as that which they had grown to love in France.

Flem said to Livy: 'Why should we go back? Mary is Queen of France.'

Livy replied that she might marry some important Frenchman. What about Charles for instance? If she married Charles she would still be Queen of France. He would marry Mary, because he had always said that he wanted to.

But Seton shook her head. 'Charles is unstable. He is only a boy. It would be quite wrong for Mary to marry him. Besides—'

The others did not ask her to continue, so Seton kept her thoughts to herself, the gist of which was that the Queen Mother would never allow such a marriage to take place.

Uncle Charles and Uncle Francis came to visit Mary while she was in her white mourning. They were very stern, but they embraced her with affection.

'This is a sad state of affairs,' said the Cardinal. 'It was a most unhappy day for our country when Francis died.'

'You must regret not being kinder to him while he lived,' Mary retorted reproachfully, for she was beginning to understand her ambitious uncles.

'There is the future to discuss,' said the Cardinal, coolly implying that he did not wish to waste time on hysterical comments.

'Shall I have to return to Scotland?' asked Mary.

'That is the last thing we wish for you.'

Mary looked relieved. 'It is the last thing I wish for,' she said. 'I love France. I look upon this country as my home. I have lived here so long. Something tells me I should never be happy in Scotland.'

'We must find you another husband,' Uncle Charles assured her.

'We have one in mind who is eager for a match with you,' Uncle Francis added. 'And I cannot think of one which would be more acceptable. If you made it you would be in the same position as you were before Francis's death.'

Mary had turned pale. 'I could not marry Charles,' she said.

'Could not marry the King of France!' thundered Uncle Charles.

'But he is so wild. At times, I think he is a little mad.'

'He is King of France,' repeated Uncle Charles, as though that settled the matter.

Uncle Francis said: 'We have another match in mind for you. The King of Spain has a son, Don Carlos. He needs a wife. How would you like to go to Spain and live with your old friend Elisabeth, who is now Queen of Spain?'

Uncle Charles was smiling. 'King Philip will not live for ever, and when he dies Don Carlos will be King, and you, my dear, his wife, would be Queen of Spain. Queen of the most powerful country in the world!'

'A pleasant prospect,' said Uncle Francis, 'but I would wish to see her Queen of France where we could be at hand.'

'To guide and comfort her,' whispered Uncle Charles affectionately.

Mary felt that she wanted to scream at them: I am mourning my husband. How dare you make use of me as though I am a piece on a chessboard!

But all she said was: 'I pray you leave me in peace.'

And they obeyed her wish.

Envoys arrived from Scotland. It was time their Queen returned to rule over them, they said.

The Queen Mother received them, for she it was who was now the most powerful person in the land, because as Charles was too young to rule she ruled for him.

'It is time the Queen of Scotland returned to her own people,' she said.

She sent for Mary. She could command her now. The young King was with her when Mary reached Catherine's apartments, and Mary knelt before him to do homage to his new status.

'Rise now, dear Mary,' said Charles. 'I am glad to see you.'

'Your Majesty is gracious,' Mary answered.

'The King has sent for you,' Catherine told her, 'to tell you that he feels that you should return to Scotland.'

Mary saw the plump hand on Charles's shoulder, holding him firmly in a grip which could well have been painful.

But Charles's face had grown purple. He said: 'I do *not* wish Mary to go to Scotland. I want her to stay here and be my Queen.'

The Queen Mother burst into that loud laughter which irritated Mary and which she now found sinister.

'My son is joking,' she said.

Charles stamped his feet. 'I do not joke,' he said. 'I will marry Mary and make her Queen, as I always said I would. Mary, you will marry me and be the Queen of France again in truth.'

'This is ridiculous,' interposed Catherine. 'The King is becoming agitated. I cannot allow that. It is bad for his health.'

'If you allow him to speak he will be less agitated,' said Mary.

'You cannot presume to tell me how to bring up my children,' said Catherine coldly. She turned to the King. 'Charles, listen to me. You are the King, but if you do not please your people and your ministers they will not allow you to keep the crown. They will set another in your place. There is your brother waiting to take the crown from you as you have taken it from Francis. They would put you in the Bastille if they decided to dethrone you, and there terrible things could happen to you. You remember I told you—'

'Do not speak of that—' cried Charles, and his face showed a terrible fear. Mary knew then that one of the ways in which the Queen Mother ruled this son of hers was by frightening him with tales of what could happen to him if he did not obey her. Mary could imagine the horrible tales Catherine told her unbalanced son, and she guessed that his sad state might well be due to his unscrupulous mother, to whose advantage it was to have him bordering on insanity.

In that moment she thought: Ought I to marry Charles? Ought I to look after him as I looked after Francis?

Both Charles and Catherine had seen the indecision in her face, and Charles called out joyously: 'Mary, you will marry me. You will!'

'Please do not be so agitated,' begged Mary.

'I am King, Mary, and I *will* marry you. You have but to say you will marry me.' He looked over his shoulder fleetingly at his mother. His look was full of fear yet it was defiant. He was so eager to marry Mary, he was telling her, that he would do so whatever his mother decided she would do to prevent him.

'You will marry when the time comes, my son,' said Catherine soothingly.

'I shall marry only Mary,' insisted Charles.

'We shall see,' murmured Catherine.

'Mary—' cried Charles.

'I am so recently widowed,' said Mary. 'I cannot think about marrying again yet. But I thank Your Majesty for your offer and I will think of it.'

Charles's face broke into a smile. 'Oh Mary,' he said. 'You will not go away then. They are trying to send you away. But they shall not. I am the King and I say so.'

Flem, who with Livy was listening in the ante-room, suddenly took her companion's hand and danced round the room with her.

'We are going to stay in France!' she whispered excitedly.

Queen Catherine sent for Mary. While she waited for her she was smiling contentedly. She had waited a long time, but now she did not mind the waiting.

She was thinking of the very first time she had seen Mary Queen of Scots. Then the little girl had not recognized her as the Queen of France and had upbraided her for coming to the nurseries. She had decided in that moment that there was a great deal she would have to teach Mary. She remembered also when she had overheard Mary refer to her as a merchant's daughter. Such slights were never forgotten by Catherine de' Medici; they were recorded in her mind and each had to be paid for.

Now the time had come for Mary to pay.

Most certainly Catherine would not allow her to marry Charles.

Catherine puffed with her lips to indicate contempt for such an idea.

No, Charles was now King and he feared his mother more than anyone else. *She* would rule Charles through fear.

As for Mary's marrying Don Carlos, that also should not come about. She had decided that her own daughter, the wayward Margot, should marry Don Carlos; then she would be sure of still having a daughter who was Queen of Spain, should Elisabeth's husband, Philip, die.

She knew in her heart that there was one thing Mary dreaded and feared above all others; and that was return to Scotland.

And Mary had very good reason to fear, for Scotland was a barbarous land compared with France. The nobles were unruly, and how would they receive a Queen who had been brought up in the elegant and fastidious Court of France, who was half-French through her mother, Mary of Guise, and was wholly so by upbringing?

Catherine knew that there was trouble brewing in Scotland where stern old John Knox was ready to rouse the Protestants – and there were many in Scotland – against the Catholic Queen.

And there was one other matter. Mary's close and powerful neighbour would be Elizabeth of England, and that Queen had reason to dislike her cousin of Scotland.

That was why, when Mary came to her presence, Catherine was purring like a cat confronted with a saucer of milk.

'Ah, my daughter.'

Mary took the extended hand with revulsion and put her lips against it as custom demanded.

'Pray be seated,' said Catherine.

Mary sat, waiting uneasily for what was to come.

Catherine did not keep her long in doubt. 'We know from the emissaries who came from your country that your subjects are eager to have you among them. I wish you to know that we would put nothing in the way of your returning.'

Mary gasped with dismay; only then did she realize how much this country meant to her, how if she were forced to leave it she would feel herself to be in exile.

'Return to Scotland?' she stammered. 'But I have no wish to do that.'

Catherine raised her eyebrows. 'It may be that your subjects will demand your return. And what is there for you in France now?'

'I have estates in France. I would retire from Court and live here in retirement.'

'We could not allow that,' murmured Catherine gently.

'I am sure the King would be pleased to allow it if I asked him.'

Catherine gave one of her unpleasant laughs. 'The King is a little indisposed. As you know, I act for him in all matters.' She puffed with her lips. 'I am sure you will be happy in Scotland. It is, after all, your country. And think how happy you will be to have as such a close neighbour your cousin of England.'

'Elizabeth is no friend of mine,' said Mary.

'But why should she not be? You are her kinswoman.'

'She will never forgive me for calling myself Queen of England.'

Mary wanted to slap the smile from Catherine's face; it contained feigned compassion and a triumph which was too great even for her to conceal.

'So not content with two crowns you had to claim a third! Ah, if you could have foreseen this day you would have acted differently.'

'I had no choice in the matter. It was the wish of the King, your husband, that I should use the title.'

'And of your uncles who were so ambitious for you. Now it is you who must take the blame.' Catherine put her hands on her hips and exploded into laughter. 'But do not fret. I am sure you will soon make the Queen of England as fond of you as you made the Queen of France.'

Mary turned away; she could endure no more.

Catherine said gently: 'You may go now. You will have a great many preparations to make since you will be leaving France.'

With a heavy heart Mary left the presence of the Queen Mother. She had received her sentence: banishment from the land which she had come to think of as her own, the land which she had learned to love.

When she had gone, Catherine de' Medici no longer attempted to control her feelings.

She laughed aloud.

Mary, one time Queen of France, self-styled Queen of England, and still Queen of Scotland, had been taught a lesson. She had been a fool ever to think she could flout Catherine de' Medici. Every insult she had dared inflict would now be paid for – in full.

So there was no hope. She was to be banished from France. Catherine ruled her son and she had decreed this to be Mary's punishment.

There were messages from Scotland. The nobles were gathering together to welcome her. They wanted their Queen to live among them, to rule over them.

The Marys were melancholy, loving France even as their mistress did.

They tried to remember what it had been like in those long-ago days of their early childhood; but it was not easy to remember, for they had only been six years old when they left.

'What I remember best of all,' Mary said to them, 'is the monastery of Inchmahome. I remember Brother Aloysius's herb garden and how the Abbot used to talk to us sometimes when we had finished our lessons.'

'Yes,' said Seton slowly, 'I remember how we used to wander to the edge of the lake and look across to the mainland, and long for someone to come and take us away – at first. Then when they came we hated saying goodbye.'

'I thought I should never be happy again when I left Inchmahome,' said Mary. 'I can remember the feeling of desolation when the time came to say goodbye. I feel it now when I must leave France.'

'So it must always be on parting,' murmured Seton.

Livy and Flem declared that they would never be happy anywhere but in France.

But Mary said softly: 'The Abbot once told me that if I

did my duty I should be happy, and I believe it is my duty to return to Scotland.'

In the harbour at Calais the galleys were preparing to leave.

On deck stood a lovely figure dressed in her mourning costume – a dress of cloth of silver, a flowing veil which cascaded over her shoulders, a headdress shaped like a scallop shell, and studded with pearls, a ruff of finest lace about her neck.

With her were her four Marys – the best consolation she could have at this time.

We came together, she thought; and we leave together.

She stood on the deck watching the coast of France as it slowly receded. She thought of all she was leaving, and the tears stung her eyes,

The life of her childhood lay behind her; who could say what the future held?

Soon she would no longer be able to see the French coast. It would not be long before she saw the coast of her own country looming through the mist.

She was overcome by sudden sadness.

Seton was at her side. 'It is cold,' she said. 'You should come below.'

She shook her head. 'I shall not leave this spot until I can no longer see the land.'

And she remained there, watching.

But the wind was strong and swiftly the ship was being carried on its way.

'It is over,' she whispered. 'Farewell beloved land which I shall behold no more! Farewell, France!'

There was no sign of the land now; it had disappeared below that line where the sea met the sky.

She turned and looked across the sea.

Ahead of her lay her new life. She was a Queen and her subjects in Scotland were waiting to welcome her.

She must find happiness now in doing her duty. She believed that if she tried to bring happiness to her people she would find what she sought. She must forget the pleasures of her life in France; Mary, the child had loved that life. But childhood did not last for ever. Now she was Mary the woman – no longer Queen of France, but Mary, Queen of Scotland and the Isles.

11

What Happened Next

Mary's life in Scotland was far from peaceful. Many enemies were waiting for her there; and she, who loved gaiety, found it difficult to conform to Scottish customs.

There was a great deal of jealousy among the nobles of her Court and, when she favoured David Rizzio, the Italian who was both politician and musician, several of them decided to murder him. Mary had married Lord Darnley, a weak and selfish young Prince, and it was not long before she regretted that marriage.

One evening when Mary was at supper, several of the nobles, among whom was Darnley, dragged Rizzio from her side and stabbed him to death.

Mary was very sad and apprehensive, believing that her enemies were planning to murder her too; she escaped from Holyrood House, helped by Lord Bothwell, a bold and ambitious man from the Border.

Soon after the escape, Mary's son was born. He was to become James VI of Scotland and James 1 of England.

One night Lord Darnley, who had been ill and was staying at a house in Kirk o' Field, died mysteriously. The house was blown up by gunpowder, but Darnley's body was found on the grass outside the house; he had escaped the explosion but was dead.

The whole of Scotland and England was asking how Darnley had died, because it seemed clear that he had been murdered, and that the explosion had been intended to suppress this fact. It was not long before people were accusing Mary and Lord Bothwell; and these suspicions increased when, very shortly after, Mary married Lord Bothwell.

The country was now split and there was war. Mary's side lost at the battle of Carberry Hill, and she was made a prisoner in the castle of Lockleven, a fortress in the middle of a loch. Here she found good friends in a young man named George Douglas and a boy, who was attached to the household, known as Willie Douglas. They helped her to escape and, realizing that there would be no peace for her in Scotland and that it would be impossible to reach France, she decided to cross the Border into England and ask Queen Elizabeth for help.

This proved to be the worst action she could have taken because Elizabeth, who had always been suspicious of Mary, was secretly delighted to have the Scottish Queen in her power.

In the beginning she pretended to treat Mary as a guest, but in fact Mary became Elizabeth's prisoner and remained so for the rest of her life, being moved from castle to castle, often living in great discomfort.

There were several attempts to bring about her escape, but all failed.

The Marys, with the exception of Seton, married; Seton stayed with Mary until she was so ill that the Queen sent her away. Seton went reluctantly, but because Mary loved her so much, she insisted on her going.

At last Mary was accused of plotting against Elizabeth, and in the Castle of Fotheringay was beheaded. She was mourned by all who had served her; and her little dog, who had hidden under her skirts when she was beheaded, refused comfort and died of grief.

Among the books which have been useful to me whilst writing this book are:

Agnes Strickland, *Lives of the Queens of Scotland and English Princesses*.
Herbert Gorman, *The Scottish Queen*.
Stefan Zweiz, *The Queen of Scots*.

With historical introduction and notes by Agnes Strickland,
  Letters of Mary Queen of Scots.

M. Guizot, *History of France*.

H. Noel Williams, *Henri II*.

Edith Sichel, *Catherine de' Medici*.

Edited by Sir Leslie Stephen and Sir Sidney Lee, *Dictionary
  of National Biography*.

If you have enjoyed this Piccolo
Book, you may like to choose
your next book from the titles
listed on the following pages.

Books by Lorna Hill in Piccolo

The adventures of Veronica Weston and her friends appear in
the famous *Sadler's Wells* series which includes

A DREAM OF SADLER'S WELLS 20p
In this poignant yet heart-warming story Veronica proves a
determined fourteen-year-old can overcome all kinds of
difficulties – even to riding horseback through fog to catch the
train for her audition.

VERONICA AT THE WELLS 20p
Veronica's ambition is to dance the Lilac Fairy at Covent
Garden, but first she must gain admission to Sadler's Wells
Ballet School.

NO CASTANETS AT THE WELLS 20p
The week Veronica left Bracken Hall was the week her cousin,
Caroline Scott, decided to slim and to take ballet seriously.
It was the first time she met Angelo Ibanez, the young
Spanish dancer.

MASQUERADE AT THE WELLS 20p
A daring deception is born when Mariella persuades Jane to
take her place at an audition for Sadler's Wells Ballet School.

Each book is complete in itself but once you've read one story
you'll want to read them all.

PICCOLO FICTION
Superb Stories – Popular Authors

FOLLYFOOT Monica Dickens 20p
Based on the Yorkshire Television Series

FOXY John Montgomery 20p

FOXY AND THE BADGERS. John Montgomery 20p

THE CHRISTMAS BOOK Enid Blyton 20p

THE OTTERS' TALE Gavin Maxwell 25p
The junior 'Ring of Bright Water'

THE STORY OF A RED DEER J. W. Fortescue 20p

FREEWHEELERS The Sign of the Beaver
  Alan Fennell 20p

PICCOLO NON-FICTION
The best in fun – for everyone

CODES AND SECRET WRITING Herbert Zim 20p

JUNIOR COOK BOOK Marguerite Patten 25p

BRAIN BOOSTERS David Webster 20p

PICCOLO QUIZ BOOK Tom Robinson 20p

FUN AND GAMES OUTDOORS Jack Cox 20p

FUN-TASTIC Denys Parsons 20p